Sunsets
and
Stables

Sunsets and Stables

A PUMPKINS & PROPOSALS NOVEL

M.K. DYMOCK

THE *Harvest Ranch Romance* SERIES BOOK 4

1

irabelle Mason stood in the setting autumn sun as the tall, dark, and handsome man knelt down, holding out a massive canary-yellow diamond. The last rays of the day set it off perfectly in a soft glow.

"Yes," she said. "Of course, yes, my love."

Mirabelle clapped along with the several others who'd been chosen to observe this carefully curated yet "spontaneous" proposal.

When the future bride, Bethany—a social media influencer with a few million followers—had reached out to Mirabelle's small stable for an event, Mirabelle had been thrilled and terrified all at once. It turned out she should've leaned more toward terrified, but the night would be over soon.

Bethany's photographer, a Frenchman named Adrien who'd helped coordinate the day, stepped up and took a series of photos of the couple and the ring. They stood on the edge of a ridge overlooking a meadow ablaze in reds and oranges with the sun setting behind the Virginia Blue Ridge Mountains.

Mirabelle allowed herself to relax for a full second. The weather had held out, the mountain views didn't disappoint, and the bride seemed happy. The proposal was part of a horseback ride she hosted a few times a week that was geared toward couples. Numbers weren't where she'd hoped they'd be, and with all her debt, she was sinking underwater fast. The weight was enough to drag anyone down, but this night could be the life preserver she so desperately needed.

All she had to do was get through the catered dinner, and the night would be over. Tomorrow, Bethany would blast her social media with the big news, tagging the stable and its romantic sunset rides. Maybe next season she'd have more sold spots than empty saddles.

"Mirabelle, darling, can you bring the horses over?" Adrien asked.

She led the horses along the ridge's edge: a white mare for the bride and a black gelding for the groom. She'd had to borrow the white one to acquiesce the future bride's request—or had it been the groom's? Bethany had first reached out about featuring the ride in a post, and then the groom had contacted her about converting the night into a surprise proposal. Though the plan had come from him, Mirabelle suspected that Bethany pulled the strings.

"Thank you ever so much," Bethany said. "It's all just so perfect. My followers are going to love you." Bethany's long dark eyelashes fluttered against her blonde hair dancing in the strong breeze.

"No, thank you." Mirabelle's face hurt from smiling so much. One more hour, she promised herself.

"Mirabelle," Bethany said. "You're still in the shot."

"Oh, sorry." She stepped back a few feet, waiting to grab the horses. While many of the pre-proposal shots had included the other couples on the ride, Mirabelle suspected she wouldn't be in them, at least not close-up. She wasn't bad-looking—even she knew that—she just wasn't influencer pretty. Her skin was more washed-out white than creamy, her freckles more chaotic than flattering, and her figure more sturdy than sexy.

While the couple finished the shoot, Mirabelle led the other couples along for the ride off the ridge and down the trail to the Dutch oven dinner prepared by the best chef in town—her uncle Jameson. He greeted all the guests while looking like an estate owner, tall with gray hair and impeccably ironed Wranglers topped with a crisp white shirt. The two other couples were friends of Mirabelle's, bribed by the promise of a free dinner, to stand in Bethany's photos and look beautiful and thrilled.

The newly engaged couple eventually sauntered into firelight about twenty minutes later to a smattering of applause. They sat on a nearby log with arms linked together, her head on his shoulder.

From where she brushed the unsaddled horses in the shadows, Mirabelle couldn't help but stare at the happy couples. How did people fall in love and stay together? From the outside, it seemed so effortless—not accounting for Bethany's engineered proposal. But from Mirabelle's experience, it seemed so impossible. She'd been engaged once—for all of two days, and that had been two days too many.

Mirabelle counted the minutes until the night was over and success could be declared. Only twenty more.

A scream echoed through the night, piercing her quiet reverie and causing her heart rate to spike. The horses jerked back on their leads, sending the trailer rocking. She leapt away to avoid their swinging rear ends.

"Where's my ring, you backwoods hillbillies? Where is it?" Bethany's accusations echoed across the mountains. She spewed several curse words—some Mirabelle had never heard.

Mirabelle rushed to the campfire, ready to take control and manage the ever-changing mood of the self-proclaimed star. "What's going on?"

"My half-million-dollar ring is missing." Bethany turned on Mirabelle, shoving her finger in her face and backing her up against her own Dodge truck. "Do you have any idea how much money that is? Of course you don't," she replied before Mirabelle could even open her mouth. "I wear more money on a single finger than you will see in your entire nothing life."

"I don't understand how it went missing." Mirabelle wouldn't let a ring like that out of her sight—not that she dated the kind of guys who had half-million-dollar rings in their pockets. Heck, the men who asked her out were lucky to have a twenty in their wallet.

"I left it with Adrien to take photos of it, and someone stole it."

Mirabelle looked to Adrien for help, but his blue eyes didn't offer a reprieve. "I had a black cloth set up to take some close-ups. I came down the hill to switch lenses. I did not know Bethany had left the—"

"I didn't *leave* the ring," Bethany shot back. "You left it, and someone stole it."

"We'll find it," Mirabelle said, and she repeated it several more times before Bethany's voice came down from shrill to terse. "Where did you see it last? I know this trail better than I know my own kitchen." She would never forgive herself for how her voice trembled in that moment.

"You'd better. That ring was an heirloom from my fiancé's great-great-grandmother."

Mirabelle glanced past Bethany to the fiancé, who looked wholly unperturbed by the missing ring and his betrothed's reaction. Maybe her response was something he'd weathered before. He took her hand. "Babe, I'm sure someone will find it."

Apparently, that someone had to be Mirabelle. She organized the guests into a search party and handed out headlamps and flashlights. They spent the next few hours hiking up and down the trail between the fire and the ridgeline where the proposal had happened, but to no avail. The strong winds of the morning returned, adding blowing leaves and dirt to the darkness.

By midnight, Mirabelle walked the still-snarling Bethany to her rented Escalade. "I'll do everything I—"

"No." Bethany held up her finger and wagged it in Mirabelle's face. "You *will* find it, because if you don't, I will grind your company to dust. I will spread the word to all my fans that you are a thief who steals from her clients. Our engagement party is one week from tomorrow, and that ring will be on my finger."

Mirabelle tried to find the words to explain that Bethany had signed a release protecting her company against lost or stolen items. She tried to find the words that it wasn't her fault the ring was lost, but she couldn't. The words didn't exist, because they didn't matter. She would never be able to afford a lawyer to fight even a baseless court case, and her tiny company could never survive the onslaught of the hate social media could bring.

"I'll find it; I promise." An infuriatingly meek voice was all she could manage. She hated herself for not being able to knock that woman to the ground.

2

Security guard Daniel Cabrera watched the crowds of the Harvest Ranch Festival with a suspicious eye. In any given group, he would expect at least ten percent will break some sort of law or rule—even if it was only littering. The one percent was who he had to worry about; they were the ones who would be doing the pickpocketing, fighting, and manhandling. At a festival in a small town such as this and it being Monday night or family night, he doubted they would see the bigger crimes, but a man could hope.

Danny used to be FBI Special Agent Cabrera, investigating financial crimes in New York City—some in the billions of dollars. Since his forced "retirement" before he'd even turned forty, he'd spent his evenings following litterbugs, issuing them citations, and cursing his circumstances every day.

"Sir," he called out, causing about twenty men to stop amongst the food booths advertising everything from donut burgers to vegan salads. "You tossed your plate on the ground."

The man in question looked around at the others as if to say, "Who, me?" The others turned their stares to the ground and slowly backed away;

they knew who the security guard meant. With no one's eyes to meet, the litterer lifted a wide-eyed, innocent gaze. "Sorry, I must've dropped it." He shrugged.

Danny had once interviewed a man who'd stolen a billion dollars and reacted with the same amount of nonchalance and lying. He hated liars, but he also knew how to handle them. "I understand, sir." He put on his most winning smile, the one his ex-girlfriend called the trap. "There aren't any garbage cans around, and you already have your hands full." He gestured to the man's other plate, which was filled with a little cabin built out of churros.

"Thank you. You would think the organizers of this thing would add more cans if they didn't want people dropping garbage on the ground."

Give a man like this a chance to blame someone else, and he would every time. Danny, with his eye on the perpetrator, very deliberately walked over to the plate, picked it up, and dropped it in the trash, a mere five feet from where they stood. "Can I see your ID?"

"Can I see your badge, Rent-a-Cop?"

As deliberately as he had picked up the plate, he pulled out his temporary badge authorizing him to work the festival on behalf of the county sheriff's office. "Sir, I understand your frustration. I don't want you to miss any more of your day than you have to." He pulled out his electronic scanner. "I'll just run your ID, and you'll be on your way."

Now that there appeared to be a chance someone was going to get in trouble, a small crowd formed around them. It always seemed to Danny the smaller the crime, the more people liked to see justice done.

The man looked around at the crowd, as if weighing how much a scene would be worth. Danny figured if he was local, he'd fight it more—not wanting to be shamed in front of his own folk. The man pulled out his ID and quickly handed it over. Danny was right—he had a South Carolina license. He quickly scanned it into his machine and printed out a ticket.

"Two hundred dollars . . . for throwing a plate! You . . ." The crowd scattered a little at the choice words the man pulled out at such an injustice.

"You have two weeks to pay it, sir." Danny added a smile as if he'd just served him an ice cream cone. He walked away, leaving the litterbug sputtering. His own smile stayed on his face. He really liked the part of the job where he gave big egos a knockdown.

Ten minutes later found him setting back up an overturned garbage can and pulling all the food scraps, bottles, and diapers back into it. He really hated this part of the job, but it was his, and he would do it well.

Only a few more months, he told himself, and he'd be back on top. He already had interviews lined up at Fortune 100 companies in their security departments. The pay would be way better than what he'd get in the public sector, and he wouldn't have to be on the road so much. Maybe, just maybe, he could finally have a normal life.

"Danny."

He glanced down the large grassy aisle separating the booths to spot Chris, his oldest and most patient friend and the sheriff of the county.

Chris walked brusquely through the crowds—or at least tried to. Every ten feet or so, he had to pause to offer a hello and send his regards to someone's mother. He finally made it over to Danny. "How's security going?"

"It's going."

Chris had gotten him this temporary gig to tide him over until he found that something better. He'd also provided him with a very small apartment over his garage. Danny found both the job and the room a huge step down from his old life—yet he still owed the man a lot. He'd offered him a refuge in a storm.

"You've got tomorrow night off, right?" Chris asked.

"Yeah, why?"

"Betsy has a friend."

"No."

"Come on, it'll be fun to go out for the night. We can double."

"Wait, I thought you were dating someone named Katie."

Chris's glance turned to watch the crowd. "We broke up. It's too hard to date a woman from the town when you're the sheriff. Betsy lives a few hours away." Chris had moved from New York a year or so ago for the job and to escape the memories of his late wife.

Unlike his friend, Danny didn't want to date just anyone to avoid an evening alone. "Any woman I go out with in this area will be looking for someone who's going to stick around, and I'm not sticky." His future lay elsewhere.

Chris offered his objections, but Danny had only one ear on the conversation as he strained to spot any suspicious behavior. A few registers had lost handfuls of cash the night before, and he was determined that it not happen again.

"Suit yourself," Chris finally offered.

A woman opened her register to make change for a twenty. She turned her back for a split second to pass on the purchased basket of chocolates when a shadow slipped out of the darkness and reached for the cash.

"I've got him," Danny said with a huge grin.

He didn't really have him, but he did get to watch the sheriff make the arrest, much to his consternation.

3

irabelle had no idea what time she slipped into bed, still covered with dust and leaves from crawling through the dirt in search of a ring that could not be found. Despite the short night, her eyes jumped open long before her body was ready.

She'd sacrificed almost everything she owned to turn her little two-acre farmhouse at the edge of the Blue Ridge Mountains into a business that could sustain her. At one point in her life, she'd worked at a job with a 401k and vacation time, counting every billable hour and saving every extra dollar. When the property had come up for sale after her engagement ended, she'd cashed in the retirement account, her savings and stocks, and pretty much every safety net she'd spent ten years acquiring.

And all of it could be gone in a second for a stupid rock worth more than all those savings combined. It was no wonder she couldn't sleep in a house still owned by the bank—twice over.

Mirabelle took fifteen minutes to shower and pull on a pair of jeans slung over her bed and a fresh shirt—she hoped. A ball cap with her curls pushed through the back saved her the time to do her hair, not that she would've done it anyhow. She and her curls had an understanding: she gave them free rein, and they did whatever they wanted, as long as they stayed out of her eyes.

Before the sun had a chance to peek over the mountains, her phone lit up with messages from Bethany. *Have you found it? Are you looking now? I'm on my way to Virginia Beach for a photo shoot for the week and then the engagement party. FIND IT BY MONDAY.*

With a piece of toast in one hand and a smoothie in the other, she locked the front door behind her and headed to her truck. As she turned the key in the ignition, she stared at everything she would spend the day trying to save. The white farmhouse carried a fresh coat of paint she'd done herself, with a bright blue door that brought her a little thrill every time she went through its threshold. While the exterior was bright and happy, she hadn't had time to do anything to the inside. Behind the house rose the old red barn—that was where most of the money had gone. It housed eight horses and ten chickens. Eventually, she wanted to expand the property and put in some tiny cabins to rent out. In the winter, there would be sleigh rides, cross-country ski trails, and romantic evenings around the fires.

But all those dreams wouldn't matter for anything if she didn't find that ring.

Mirabelle desperately hoped that with the full light of morning, the ring would appear in all its sparkling glory and she would spot it.

But it didn't, and she couldn't.

By ten, she stood at the small county sheriff's office across the street from the festival, explaining her story to Sheriff Calvetti—a man with a salt-and-pepper beard who'd moved to town after she'd left it for college.

"We can certainly fill out a report if you think it was stolen. Are you sure no one took it?" He looked at her expectantly.

"Yes, I'm sure. She left it on a rock, and everyone else was back at the campfire eating."

"Sounds like it might pay off to find someone with a metal detector. I think we've got one I could lend you. I'll drop it off later today."

"Yeah, thanks." She turned to the door, her feet dragging.

"You know, I'd head to the festival and talk to the security guards there."

"Why?"

"You can fill out a missing item report and post some flyers and such. We've got thousands of people in town for the festival and all over the mountains during the next few weeks. Ask for Danny; he's new to the area and would love to help you."

"No." Mirabelle heard the underlying message. She'd had her fill of everyone in this town—challenged by her single status—trying to set her up on dates with every available man between twenty and fifty.

"You sure? He just retired from the FBI and would love to sink his teeth into something like this."

Her hackles lowered, and her clenched shoulders softened. An old, retired guy was well beyond the age limit of being a threat to her quiet Friday nights. "What's his name again?" As much as she was loathed to admit it, she really did need help.

* * * * *

Danny arrived at the small windowless building that served as head-quarters for the five security guards whom he'd quite enjoyed training. They were all fresh out of high school and bent on earning a quick buck. The city had put him in charge of the feeble crew, and he would make adults out of them.

He went behind the counter and pulled out the reports from the night before to see what else had gone on. Other than the few teenagers who'd grabbed the cash, a couple of drunk guys kicking over garbage cans, and a raccoon that had somehow locked itself in a bathroom, not much had happened.

The door creaked open, and in walked a woman straight from the country, her boots caked in mud and a stain of unknown origin on her jeans. A cascade of brown curls sprang out the back of her trucker ball cap, worn completely unironically. The hipsters in New York would pay good money for her look, which he suspected had been thrown on without a second thought—a quality he both judged and secretly envied.

Danny unconsciously brushed his pants and pulled down the cuffs of his uniform. His Army father had drilled into him the importance of first impressions. "Being the son of an immigrant, people will judge you from the moment they meet you," he'd said many times. "You don't have the luxury of a second impression like others do."

Danny straightened up and greeted the woman with a smile. "How can I help you?" He offered a smile, because that was what he always did—friend or foe. He'd sort out who was who later.

She shot him a disappointed look, and he leaned toward classifying her as foe. With a sigh, she said, "My name is Mirabelle Mason. I run a stable in town, and I do sunset horse rides in the mountains." She did not offer him a smile back, but her light-brown eyes held a depth of exhaustion. "Last night, one of my guests lost her engagement ring. The sheriff told me to ask for Danny."

Chris had sent this woman to him. He immediately stood straighter and retracted the smile. His old friend should be more worried about his own single status than Danny's. "Where and when did she last have it?" He forced a disinterested a tone, not wanting to give the woman the wrong idea.

"Last night around seven up on Rocky Ridge. She'd taken it off to get some pictures of it. When the photographer went back, the ring was gone."

"Stolen?"

"No," she pounced before he'd finished the word. Interesting. "It probably fell in the dirt or she forgot where she set it down. It was dark, and there were strong wind gusts last night."

He took in her grubby appearance. "I take it you've looked all morning?"

She looked a little surprised by his precognition. "Yeah, I looked everywhere."

"Then it's stolen."

"No," she said firmly, her now-alert eyes warned him from arguing the point.

Her challenging look caught him off guard, and he gave her a second glance. He was used to CEOs of thousands of employees pushing back against his accusations, but not stable hands. Her eyes held a sense of confidence and a dare to question her. He found himself, rather unprofessionally, wanting to challenge her and to win.

If Chris did have a nefarious purpose in sending her to him, she was not in on it.

"Why not?" he asked.

"I personally know everyone who was at that dinner, and no one, and I mean no one, would've stolen it."

He'd once investigated the theft of ten million dollars from a family trust. The money had been transferred out and into a series of accounts it'd taken weeks to trace. The family had blamed the lawyers of the trust, certain that no relative would steal from them. He'd traced the money to the seventy-year-old matriarch, who had a secret gambling addiction.

"If it had been lost or misplaced, wouldn't you have found it?" He picked up a pad of paper and wrote down a few notes.

She flashed a split second of doubt before she shook her head. "Maybe not. A squirrel could've thought it was a nut and carried it away."

He laughed out loud. "A squirrel?"

She took a step closer, her brown eyes ablaze, and he found himself taking a step back. "People in town for the festival are going to be hiking all over the mountains taking photos. All I need is for you to put up some flyers. Can you do that?"

Danny smoothed back his dark hair and debated how to reset the conversation. Something about this woman told him she wouldn't give him the upper hand. "Of course." He used his most congenial voice to bring her back to his side, but one look at her set jaw told him that wouldn't get him far, and he dropped it. "But if it is lost in the forest and not stolen, your chances of finding it are slim to none."

"Look, that ring is an heirloom worth a half-million dollars. I have to find it."

Danny's pen stopped mid-word. He pulled his eyes up to meet hers. "How much did you say?"

The morning might prove to be more entertaining than he'd thought possible.

When the sheriff had told Mirabelle to ask a retired FBI agent for help, she'd pictured a gray-haired stoic figure. She hadn't expected the way-too-sure-of-himself younger man in a perfectly pressed uniform. Sure, he was good-looking in one of those dark and brooding ways, but not enough to warrant his arrogance.

She knew men like him. She'd been engaged to a man like him before thinking better of it. Now she avoided men like him.

Yet, despite her protestations that she really didn't need his help, she found herself driving him to the ridge in her truck. Nothing but the absolute terror of losing her business would allow her to acquiesce to that. Let him look around and, if he couldn't help, she would send him on his way. And if he found the ring? She would say thank you and then still send him on his way.

"Why isn't the person who lost the ring the one looking for it?" he asked.

She couldn't pinpoint his accent beyond Northern and abrasive, but it put her on the defensive. "She has a photoshoot at the ocean."

"Why doesn't she file a police report if it's worth so much?"

"I don't know. She didn't leave much room for me to ask questions. Either I find the ring, or she destroys my company." Mirabelle shifted down as the truck started up the steeper grade. The gears ground, and she shoved it harder.

He clutched the side of the door as the tires climbed over some rocks. "Can she do that?" he asked between gritted teeth.

"She has a million followers. It doesn't have to be true; it just has to go viral."

"Tell me about last night. You mentioned other people being there. Wouldn't a proposal be more of a private thing?"

"I did offer her fiancé a private event for the two of them, but he'd said Bethany would want an audience." She clenched the steering wheel tighter, remembering all the requirements she'd been given in the weeks leading up to it. "She insisted on vetting everyone, meaning only people who would be comfortable in front of a camera, i.e. good-looking and would sign a photo release."

"Wait, I thought the fiancé was planning a surprise proposal?"

"*Surprise* is a loose term. She planned the night, but the ring was his idea, supposedly."

"Why did you agree to it?" Skepticism crept out of his voice.

"Why?" Her voice rose in the small cab. "Because I have a business to run, and a good word from her would—or would've, before everything went pear-shaped—sold a lot of empty spots this season and into next."

"I only meant she sounds demanding to work with."

"Demanding? Do you know what I've been through the last weeks trying to make that woman happy?" Her pent-up rage over the last few days spewed out on this man. Better him, she supposed, than her loved ones. "I'd invited one couple I've been friends with for years, and I had to disinvite them. Care to know why?"

His expression said he didn't want to know why, but bless his heart, he answered, "Why?"

"Bethany didn't think their vibe matched the tone of the night. I don't think she appreciated that my friend was runner-up to Miss Virginia. The only reason she let my best friend, Tamyra, come along—who's also gorgeous—was because she liked the idea of 'diversity of race' in her photos.

Her words, not mine."

Mirabelle had warned Tamyra about the influencer's comment, but she'd come anyway out of support for her and general kindness. Kindness, however, hadn't precluded Tamyra from crossing her eyes in every photo she could without being noticed. Mirabelle had to finally walk away from the shoot for a few minutes and laugh out loud in the trees.

Danny stretched his legs out in the passenger side, thinking on something he wasn't telling her. In the coolness of the day, she could feel the warmth radiating off his body. She leaned closer to the door, uncomfortable at being this close to a strange man—especially a decent-looking strange man.

She took a breath. "Sorry to spill this on you. It's just been a long month prepping, and it still all went wrong. I'm just glad I'm not part of the wedding planning."

While she regretted taking her anger out on an innocent bystander, she would still keep her guard up. She didn't get a vibe that this city man was interested in her, but she'd better keep things professional just the same. Didn't want there to be any misunderstanding on his part.

"How many people ended up being there besides the engaged couple?" he asked.

"Two couples on the ride and my uncle Jameson doing the cooking. Bethany had wanted three couples accompanying—one couple at the start of their relationship, one in the middle, and another together for a lifetime." She sighed at the last part. "My aunt was supposed to come but wasn't feeling well."

The truck lurched over the last few rocks, and she pulled into the yellowing grass alongside the four-wheel drive road, parking. She stepped out into mud, still deep from the previous morning's storms. "This is where we had a campfire."

Danny followed suit more gingerly. With his fancy leather shoes and no hat, he definitely did not belong here. Most men she knew had an everyday ball cap, a dress-up ball cap, and cowboy hat for rodeos and nicer occasions. Her former fiancé hadn't worn hats.

She shook her head. Like this city man had any chance of finding a tree in this forest—let alone a tiny yellow rock. "I don't know what you think you're going to find; I've been all over this area."

He ignored her question. "Show me where the ring was last seen."

Last seen? What were they in, some crime caper movie? "I still don't see how it could be stolen," she said, remembering his comment back at the festival.

His breathing grew heavy as she led him up the trail to the ridgeline. Lowlanders always struggled up here.

"They were shooting it on that rock there." She pointed out a black boulder that had been a strong contrast with the yellow ring.

He walked over and squatted in front of it. Nothing to find there, she knew.

"There were so few of us," she continued. "You'd have to be stupid to take something when you're for sure going to get blamed for it."

He stood up. "What makes you think they're smart?"

"So my friends are stupid and criminals?" This was a waste of time. She'd borrow that metal detector and find it herself.

"That ring didn't walk off by itself. Besides, your theory of a squirrel mistaking it for a nut seems highly unlikely. It was stolen."

He really thought her an idiot. "That was one of a hundred possibilities other than someone stealing it."

"What are the other hundred?"

Her mouth opened, but nothing came out. The only ideas that flooded her brain were raccoon, chipmunk, or some other critter that would only bring on more mocking.

"Then we have to consider it was stolen," he continued, walking to the edge of the ridge. "I'll want to talk to everyone there last night."

"I don't need your help anymore," she finally sputtered. Bethany had threatened to take down her company. She'd let that happen before she'd allow a stranger to accuse her friends and family of a crime.

He took a step toward her, his almost black eyes piercing hers. "I'll give you one day," he said as if bequeathing her a giant favor. "You want to lose your business?"

His close proximity was more than a little flummoxing. She shook off that feeling like she'd shaken off another man who'd stood in the way of building her life here. Mirabelle hadn't needed him, and she was loath to rely on anyone else. However, the two mortgages she owed at the first of each month didn't really care who helped her.

She pressed her lips together, considering her options and if she really needed his help. "I don't know . . ."

"What are you afraid of? If no one has anything to hide . . ." A smile transformed his face from smirking to charming, and that sudden change worried her more than anything.

5

As much as Danny wanted to, he really shouldn't give any more time to this woman. When he wasn't at the festival, he ought to be on the computer chasing down leads on a job—not leads on a missing ring. Doing something for nothing, or at least very little, was his old world. Watching men with all the power constantly walking out of jail with a fine and a "please don't do it again" had driven him to a breaking point.

Now broken, he didn't need to help anyone besides himself.

But something about a woman losing her half-million-dollar engagement ring and not contacting the police or even broadcasting it all over her social media didn't sit right with him. The investigator inside him had stirred, and he always had a hard time shutting him down.

He and Mirabelle continued along the ridgeline where the proposal had happened and the ring had disappeared. The view took in a small meadow surrounded by trees slipping into the reds and oranges of fall. A low haze hung over the Blue Ridge Mountains rising all around them. As much as he missed New York and its bustling streets, he had to admire this beauty.

"It's something, isn't it? Another week and this'll all be brown. We're already past peak colors." Mirabelle had slipped in beside him. "I plan it so that the ride ends here right in time for the sunset. That's when the proposal happened."

"Walk me through exactly what went down leading up to that moment."

Mirabelle recited the events from the start of the evening to the campfire scream. "Each ride begins at my house, where we saddle up and take some photos. Then Uncle Jameson drives up here to get dinner prepared while we ride about six miles to this ridge."

"How did the ring go missing?"

"I guess Bethany left it for Adrien to shoot. Everyone was sitting around the fire when she came down. I don't know how anyone could've gotten to it."

She was circling the wagons around her friends—already trying to protect them without knowing for sure their guilt or innocence. How many times had he witnessed that happening? Some might call him cruel, but he kind of loved that moment when the person who swore their brother, cousin, or friend would never do such a thing realized they had indeed done the thing. Then it was even odds which way it would go down. The loved one would either dig deeper in denial or collapse at the realization they didn't know their family so well.

Which way would Mirabelle go? It would be interesting to see.

"Anyways," Mirabelle continued, "I can assure you none of them stole it."

She would probably go deeper in denial, but maybe she'd surprise him. "I'm sure," he said, barely trying to conceal his sarcasm. He would help her. He didn't have any job interviews for a few days, and things at the festival picked up more at night. After that, she was on her own—if he hadn't found the ring already.

Although he had to admit he was a little more handicapped than usual. Danny was used to having the world's most cutting-edge investigative tools at his fingertips. In seconds, he could've run background checks on each of the night's participants and known more about them than their own spouses would ever know.

"I'd like to go down and get that metal detector, if you don't mind, and come back up," Mirabelle said.

He could tell by her tone she didn't really care if he did mind. "Do you have a ride tonight?" he asked.

"No, only Thursday through Saturdays. Monday was special for Bethany."

Ten minutes later, he stretched his legs out in the surprisingly clean truck cab. Nothing about the vehicle reflected its chaotic owner. He pulled out a pen and a notebook, wishing he had his iPad. "You said no one left the fire when the ring went missing?"

"Nope."

The bumps of the road sent his pen scraping across the paper. "Were you at the fire? Before, you mentioned you were seeing to the horses when you heard her scream."

She shifted on the seat and kept her eyes on the "road" ahead. "Yeah, but I was only a few feet away from everyone."

"How many feet?"

"Just twenty. Thirty at most," she added rather reluctantly.

"And it was dark?"

"Yeah."

He didn't push her anymore, recognizing how quickly she'd turn into a reluctant witness. It always amazed him how many people didn't act in their own best interest in an investigation. He'd seen suspects being investigated for murder still lie about not having an alibi to cover up an affair. As if the FBI would never figure that out.

He watched Mirabelle out of the corner of his eye, wondering what stuff she'd try to hide. A little thrill coursed through him as he imagined what fun it would be to figure it out. He liked a challenge, and something about her said she'd be all that and then some.

She was in her thirties, a business owner, no ring on her finger, and no mention of a husband or boyfriend. Going by her treatment of him, she had no desire to change that. Most single women at least offered him a smile and a warm "hello." She barely glanced at him. Not that he considered himself God's gift to women, but he had a job, a full head of black hair, and was in decent shape, which for a single guy in his thirties was usually all it took to garner a second glance.

Except he no longer had a job. He glanced down at his khaki uniform that made Boy Scouts look well dressed. Maybe that kept Mirabelle at bay. Yet another reason his stint in this town would have to be temporary. Another sacrifice he made for the FBI was that of a decent relationship, and he was determined not to hit forty alone.

"You know, I don't need you to come back with me," Mirabelle said. "The sheriff said I could borrow his metal detector."

He somehow suspected his uniform wasn't the sole reason for her lack of flirting. "Good, I'm not planning on it."

"What are you planning on?" she asked suspiciously.

"Talking to everyone who was there that night and seeing if their stories match up."

"Match up to what?"

"Yours, for starters. Each other's as I learn more."

She opened and closed her mouth, definitely not liking his plan. "There is one person you can talk to."

He leaned closer, curious as to who she would offer as a sacrificial lamb.

"Bethany brought her own photographer. He had his eyes and camera on everything that night."

"Good, I'll talk to him first." He emphasized the word "first."

She sighed. "I'd better go with you."

"Not necessary." He didn't want her standing around with her glares controlling the conversation.

"Not negotiable."

He looked away from her and out the window, trying to hide his grin. Today would be fun.

* * * * *

Desperate to keep Danny away from anyone she cared about and Bethany, Mirabelle called the only person she wasn't worried about him offending—Adrien, the photographer. "Bella, darling," he said before she could say hello. "Have you managed to apply lotion to that huge burn Bethany gave you?"

Bluetooth had automatically sent the call through her truck's speakers. She smashed a few buttons on her phone in a futile attempt to turn it off. "I wasn't . . ."

"Don't pay any attention to that woman. She only insults those she's intimidated by."

With a glance at Danny, who was very much listening in, she took a deep breath. "Then you'd think I would be safe."

"Don't be silly. She does not like other self-made women. She thinks you are all competition."

Next to her, Danny cleared his throat.

"I wanted to talk to you about the ring," Mirabelle said.

"Of course. Do you want to meet up for a late lunch?"

"Wait, you're still in town?"

"Of course. Bethany didn't only threaten your job. If I lose her business, I lose half my income for the year. More with all the photography that will go along with the wedding."

"Tell him yes," Danny leaned in to whisper.

She waved him off. "There's a café in town called Blue Shadow. We can meet there in a half hour."

"Very good."

She hung up, only to be swamped in Danny's disapproving glare. "I take it I'm supposed to invite you?" she said.

"Only if you want to find the ring." His gaze lingered a little longer on her, and she glanced down at her clothes.

"Oh, crap." That was an apt term for the clothing she'd thrown on that morning without any thought besides not being naked. The last time she'd worn these jeans, she'd been mucking out the stalls. If only she'd suggested the other café in town, where all the farm and outdoor folks ate as they were. Blue Shadow was a cutesy place done up for the tourists, which was why she'd thought of it.

As if reading her thoughts, Danny spoke up. "We can stop at your house."

Did she smell so bad he wouldn't deign to be seen with her? Well, forget him. His uniform was pressed so hard she could cut her finger on its seam. Still, though, she did have a professional meeting. Adrien had offered to shoot around the stables to create some advertising.

They pulled into her driveway with gravel spraying up from the mud tires. She glanced at her watch. "Give me fifteen minutes."

Mirabelle had mastered the ability to shower, dress, and throw on mascara in less time than it took to saddle a horse. Every once in a while, she forced herself to take a full half hour, but she usually couldn't discern any measurable change in her appearance to make the extra time worthwhile.

She left Danny in the yard, not trusting him to not rummage through her house the second he could. He wouldn't find anything besides a whole lot of bills she may not be able to pay and a saddle she was retooling in the living room.

Two minutes faster than predicted, she stepped out on her porch to find her yard in disarray, meaning it was more organized than ever before. Somehow in the short time, he'd straightened the rocking chairs on the porch, cleaned out a few flowerpots, and started to rake the bright red leaves from the dogwood tree into a neat pile.

"What the . . .?" She'd been right not to let him into her home.

To her surprise, he glanced up with a smile that transformed his face into someone she might not have disliked in her old life. "Sorry, I don't do well sitting still."

Neither did she. A tirade sat on the tip of her tongue, aching to be released, but what did she have to complain about? She'd been meaning to do all those things but had set them aside for other priorities. Not sure how to respond, she simply walked past him and climbed into the truck.

"How much do you know about the photographer?" Danny asked after he climbed in the passenger seat.

"He's from France. Bethany met him on a vacation and said he's a genius." Going by some of the photos she'd seen, she was apt to believe Bethany on that front. He had an artistic eye that brought even the most boring of shots to life. "I doubt he'd steal the ring. She'd destroy him too."

Danny settled into the seat and jotted down more notes. At least her truck was immaculate. She had to put all her focus on anything that guests would see. Her barn was cleaner than her bedroom.

Before he could put his seat belt on, her hand hit her forehead. "I forgot my cell phone."

Ten minutes later, they were pulling out again. "A ring worth half a million dollars would entice a lot of people," he continued. "He wouldn't need a career then."

Danny was right, she hated to admit. Not necessarily about Adrien, but about motive. She considered what she could buy with 500K. Forget buying; think of the bills she could pay off. "How would you even sell it?"

The truck hit a hole in the dirt road, which sent Danny's pen across the paper. The sight of a jagged line through his perfect penmanship caused her a small amount of glee. "Not easily," he admitted. "And you wouldn't get the full value on the black market. You'd have to know someone."

Her imagination cut one of the two mortgages for the farm off her list. "You're saying some experienced criminal managed their way onto my romantic horseback ride to steal it. Or someone stole it with no way to actually sell it."

He glanced at her. "Is that less believable than your squirrel with rich tastes using it as part of his nest?"

She'd never wanted to stick her tongue at someone so much since elementary school, when Joey Jarvis had called her a skinny boy and she'd punched him. With the same fight in her, she shot back, "If you were an FBI agent, why are you here? Are you undercover working the mystery of the squirrel gang? Is this not their first heist?"

He flinched, and she knew her shot aimed true. Guilt seeped in to darken her victory, but she forced it back.

Danny shifted in his seat and stared out the window at the changing leaves rushing by. "I needed to deal with some personal issues."

That was the same line Mirabelle had told people when she'd quit her job in finance. Her actual truth—a broken engagement—had her questioning every part of her life. She wondered what his truth was. *Keep it professional,* she reminded herself. Instead of asking, she turned up the radio on an old Glen Campbell song, and they drove the rest of the way in silence.

The sooner they found the ring, the sooner she could be free of him.

6

big part of why Danny had joined the FBI was a desire to right the wrongs of a world destined to favor the rich. But the reason he'd succeeded so well was a love of taking what appeared to be chaos and making sense of it.

While Mirabelle Mason wasn't necessarily the first, she definitely embodied the latter. He couldn't make sense of her, and for that reason—and no other, he told himself—his mind would not stop stewing over her.

She went in ten different directions all at the same time. Even as they drove, she fielded calls about the current week's "rides," as she referred to them. Her clothes, while now clean, were still in disarray. She'd pulled one pant leg over a boot with the other stuffed in. Her ball cap sat crooked. Before they even passed her gate, she'd gone back into the house for her phone, sunglasses, and keys—all separate trips.

Danny never left the house without being fully prepared for every contingency, even in an emergency. How did she make it out the door? He wasn't so much judgmental about it, but very, very confused. He pulled up countless reviews on her business, heralding her for her organizational skills. *Every detail planned to perfection on the most romantic night of our lives,* read one review and echoed in many others.

Maybe the chaotic personality was a cover for stealing the ring? Let him think she was incapable of such a crime? He didn't quite believe it, but he couldn't put it past her until he knew more about her.

That was the answer. He needed to know more about her. She would be the key to solving this thing. Either it was her, or it was someone she knew. After all, she'd claimed several times how well she knew each and every guest that had been there that night.

The truck hit another bump, and his fingers slipped off the buttons as he typed her name into his Yelp app. He swore she kept doing that on purpose, but for what reason he couldn't fathom. A sly little smile crept over her face, and her foot never touched the brake. She wasn't fooling him.

He chose to ignore that for now. "After the ring went missing, how long did your friends stay after and help?" he asked. He wondered if one of them had stumbled onto the ring lost in the dirt and had held on to it. Maybe it was a crime of opportunity or even a little comeuppance to an uppity outsider.

"A couple of hours, but the dark didn't allow for too much searching. They would've stayed all night," she added somewhat defensively.

"It's good to have friends like that." He brushed a bit of dust off his shoe. "It's strange coming to a new place and not knowing a soul."

Her grip on the wheel softened somewhat. "You're friends with the sheriff, right?"

"Since we were eight and realized fighting everyone else was way more fun than fighting each other."

She snuck a glance from the road to him, seizing him up. "And if somebody accused him of stealing, would you believe them?"

He didn't answer right away, giving the question some thought as he stared at the varying shades of green pines speeding past the window. "I wouldn't necessarily believe them, but I'd investigate. One thing I've learned is that no one knows someone as well as they think they do. Everyone has something they want to keep private—whether it's a hidden family or a stash of chocolate in the back of the pantry."

"Fine," she said after a moment. "Investigate them. You'll see nobody I know had anything to do with it. We're more 'chocolate in the pantry' people."

They stayed in silence the rest of the way until they pulled into the parking lot of a picturesque café surrounded by changing trees and a few evergreens. Cars lined the road and filled the parking lot out back.

All the storefronts on Main Street were done up to resemble the Scandinavian villages of the town's forefathers, with faux windmills and second-story wooden balconies. Between that and the cowboy-themed name, Harvest Ranch, the town appeared to be suffering from an identity crisis.

"Is it always this crowded?" he asked.

"No, it's totally due to the festival. It used to be a small local event for farmers to sell their goods, but now . . ." She shook her head. "All it took was a few Instagram shots of the mountain fall colors behind the pumpkin races, and next thing you knew, we were a destination."

He couldn't tell by the tone of her voice if that was a bad thing or a good thing. "That's why the sheriff called me," Danny said. "He said the last few years the crowds have gotten so big, their little force couldn't keep up with it. He gave me the okay to hire temp guys for the month."

"Are you all right helping me today?"

Her tone seemed sincere, and he appreciated her concern. "Oh yeah, the day shift is pretty quiet with mostly families and such. The night gets a little crazier, but I have tonight off." *Crazy* being a subjective term. Beyond a few drunk brawlers and shoplifters, he hadn't done too much policing, which had him bored to tears.

Giving up on the parking lot, Mirabelle found a space a street over. She spent a few minutes trying to wedge the Dodge diesel into a spot better suited for a Mini Cooper.

"I don't know if . . ."

"I got this." She craned the wheel all the way to the right and parked within an inch of the truck's life, not to mention the other car's.

"Impressive."

"You don't need to be sarcastic," she shot at him.

He leaned back at the surprise tirade. "I was being serious. I lived in New York. If I had tried that in that city with this beast, I would've killed three pedestrians, two bikers, and probably some poor homeless person in a wheelchair."

"Oh, sorry." She didn't make eye contact and slipped out the door and out of sight.

He followed Mirabelle up the street—all pride but not a lot of confidence out of the mountains. She kept her eyes on the concrete. Definitely not the same woman who'd led him up a trail with sure strides and a loping gait.

They rounded the corner back to Main Street, and it still surprised him. When Danny had first come to town, he'd found the Scandinavian theme a bit over the top, but he'd grown to appreciate the deep roots of the settlers that set it apart from the neighboring areas. And then he spotted the café, which had taken those inviting Swiss details and pumped them up by ten. The hostess who greeted them, along with all the waitstaff, wore lederhosen, with the women in thick petticoats under skirts. He had to wonder if they yodeled for birthdays.

The hostess walked them to a table outside on the patio next to some outdoor heaters designed to take the edge off the autumn chill. They passed a large group as a waitress announced a birthday. Yes, they yodeled with a pitch Danny hadn't known was possible.

A handsome blond-haired man with a camera stood at their approach and ignored Mirabelle's outstretched hand to envelope her in a hug. She awkwardly patted his back before sitting back, her face three shades redder than it had been.

Adrien, the photographer, turned his blue eyes to Danny but luckily didn't refuse his handshake in favor of a hug. Danny sucked in his gut and rolled his shoulders back to gain more height over the shorter man. Despite his slight height advantage, he figured Adrien's arms were twice the size of his. He reminded himself to be genial to get the man talking. Always be the suspect's friend—until you were their enemy.

"Danny here," Mirabelle said, gesturing to him, "worked with the FBI, so he's helping me find the ring."

Adrien's eyes widened a bit. Out of guilt? "How fascinating. Were you one of those advisors like you see on TV who help with cases?" He spoke with a faint accent and perfect English.

"No, I'm an agent . . . was an agent." That terse statement couldn't be further from genial.

Adrien must've sensed the awkwardness and turned to Mirabelle. "Belle, love. When are we going to shoot your farm? I cannot imagine a more idyllic setting for autumn. I want to capture it before it's gone." He turned to Danny. "Can you picture a better setting or woman for a shoot? With her coloring, she's the embodiment of fall."

Mirabelle dropped another few degrees of redness into a shade he wouldn't have thought possible. He hated how quickly women were taken in by flattering words from a man with clearly no substance. He'd thought her made of stronger stuff.

Then he remembered he barely knew her. Adrien could claim his territory all he wanted; Danny had no interest in a woman who would be charmed by this guy. "I suppose not."

"Adrien," Mirabelle interrupted. "There won't be a farm if we don't get that ring back to Bethany, nor will you have a job."

The photographer's face dropped at this unwelcome reminder. "You are right. Photographs of beautiful settings won't matter with no reputation. Bethany has been calling constantly this morning for an update."

"Better you than me," Mirabelle muttered.

Adrien's charming persona immediately retracted like a snake back in its hole, replaced with all business. "How do you plan to find it?" he asked Danny.

"By finding the person who stole it."

Adrien's eyes barely lifted. "Who do you believe that is?" He didn't ask why Danny believed it was stolen.

"That's what I hope to find out. When was the last time you saw the ring?"

Adrien didn't answer for a moment. Whether he was weighing his answer or weighing Danny, he couldn't say. "We'd created a setting on a rock overlooking the valley with the sun behind it. I probably shot it at ten different angles and a few hundred images."

"Could you send me those with timestamps?"

"Of course. I left the ring on the rock to go get a different flash. I wanted a few pictures in the low light."

"You left a half-million-dollar ring sitting out unattended?" Geniality had long fled. Danny always struggled with the so-called charmers. To get cooperation, it was usually better to pretend their skills worked, but he hated giving them that satisfaction. Still, he was usually better at this. Something about this guy set him off. Maybe it was Mirabelle blushing at his flattery and only glaring at him. Interested in him or not, she'd pricked his pride.

She shot him a warning look to back off, which he ignored.

Adrien straightened. "No, I left an engagement ring in the presence of the intended bride. When I went back, it was gone. I'd assumed she had it, but when I went down to ask her, we realized it was missing."

"How long between when you left the ring and went back?"

Adrien looked to Mirabelle as if she could provide him an answer. "Was that when we spoke about the shoot?"

"No, that was before you took the first photos," she said.

He scrunched up his ridiculously good-looking face. "Maybe ten minutes. I couldn't find the flash amongst my bags."

Danny eyed the Frenchman up. How easy would it have been to slip the ring into one of his camera bags? He clearly had a passport and could be out of the country before anyone could stop him. A half-million dollars could go a long way anywhere.

A fairly perfect crime, except for one thing. Adrien hadn't actually gotten on a plane, and he was willingly talking to an FBI agent. Okay, former agent, but still. "Why didn't Bethany call the police?" He'd asked the same question of Mirabelle, but she hadn't had a decent answer.

Adrien leaned forward as if about to confess. "The ring is an heirloom from the fiancé's family."

Danny noticed no one ever called the groom-to-be by his name. He wondered if his name didn't matter that much.

"They offered it to him for another girl he was dating last year—hand-picked by the mother and a family friend. But once Bethany set her sight on him, that other girl didn't last very long. The family hates her for that. I don't think she dares admit she lost the ring within an hour of receiving it."

"But what about the fiancé? Doesn't he care the ring was lost?"

Adrien waved his hand in disregard. "Bah, he's so rich, I don't think he knows the difference between the price of milk and a family heirloom."

"So why is she so desperate to get it back?"

"Because the family will notice, and they control the money, not him. He may be clueless, but Bethany is not."

"Could Bethany . . .?" Mirabelle pondered the words.

"Bethany steal it?" Adrien scoffed. "That diamond is nothing compared to the fortune that awaits her. All that girl needs are a ring and a baby, and she's set for life. Several lives, in fact. If she doesn't get it back, she'll do whatever it takes to place the blame on someone else."

"And that includes you and Mirabelle?" Danny asked.

Adrien shot a sympathetic glance at Mirabelle. "Mostly Mirabelle. I helped build Bethany's brand and her reputation; she trusts me. She may fire me for a time, but she won't destroy me." He said this without pride but a sense of grudging acceptance. "But the bigger she gets, the more power she has over my career."

Danny had spent a lot of time investigating the crimes of rich people stealing from other rich people. It used to bother the other agents to put so much effort into people who wouldn't miss the money, but it didn't bother him. A crime was a crime. What did bother him was how often those crimes got blamed on someone without power to defend themselves.

It bothered him so much, in fact, it had cost him his badge. Mirabelle had no idea the kind of people she was up against. This Bethany could squash her and not even notice the mess on her stiletto.

Maybe he'd give this more than just the day.

irabelle jingled her keys as they walked back to the truck, deep in thought. The more Danny insisted someone had stolen the ring, the more she dug in that no one at her dinner would've. He had to be wrong; he didn't know this town like she did.

Danny wasn't one to let her stay in those thoughts too long. "Why do you think Adrien's still in town?" he asked.

"Partly on Bethany's behalf and partly on his own. He said he wanted to get shots of the festival and the mountains. Most of his photography revolves around her. I think he wants to broaden his portfolio." She stopped at the corner and turned around, unsure of exactly where she'd parked the truck.

"That's not all he wants to broaden."

"What's that mean?" She swore she'd parked on Sycamore Street.

"The truck is this way," Danny said, pointing down Maple Street.

"Are you sure?" She didn't really question his knowledge but was bothered by him knowing her town better than her.

"When you're in law enforcement, you always know where your vehicle is."

"Fair enough." The town's small commercial district gave way to colonial houses made with stones quarried from the mountain. Those homes had been there long before them and would be there long after. "What did you mean about Adrien wanting to broaden? Do you think he stole the ring? Wouldn't that mean he'd be eager to leave?"

"Maybe, but you're probably right about him not stealing it," he said.

Ha, she was right about something around this know-it-all.

"I mean, he's clearly putting the moves on you."

Mirabelle so stunned, she stopped in the middle of Maple Street. A minivan tooted its horn, and she jogged to the sidewalk. "That is the stupidest thing I've ever heard. Are you sure you're good at investigating?"

"He was flirting with you quite heavily."

"He's French, and it comes out like that. He would act the same if I was eight or eighty. Ninety percent of what he says is pure BS. Take his wanting to photograph me. That's just a line so I'll go along with his having a photoshoot at the farm, which I'm totally fine with."

Danny picked up his step and matched her stride. "I totally agree."

"Gee, thanks." Mirabelle knew she wasn't going to get a second career as a model, but the polite thing was not to agree so heartily.

"No—I mean, yes . . ." Danny fell silent.

It was a good thing her self-esteem wasn't reliant on this man—or really, any man. At least it hadn't been for a while. She'd occasionally felt the pain of loneliness with no relationship in sight. She had no regrets, though. Every time she felt the need to pair up, she'd remind herself of everything she had going for her: a family who loved her, a farm that could be on a postcard, and a growing business.

Except Bethany had threatened the last two.

"Where are we going to now?" Danny asked.

"We?"

"I thought we could visit more of the people who were there last night."

She sighed, still not sure she wanted him around folks she actually cared about. Did she really need his help that much?

"What are you so worried about?" he asked. "If they're innocent like you swear up and down they are, then I won't find anything."

"If you come after my loved ones . . ."

He put his hands up. "I won't unless there's very clear evidence."

"Fine. My uncle Jameson does the cooking for the evening rides. He's smarter than me by three and a lot more observant. That night I was too busy running around making sure everything went well." She hesitated a moment. "Obviously, I failed. Anyhow, I was fixing to go over there and pick his brain."

"There's your truck." He pointed down the street, where the large tank sat innocently waiting. Stupid thing must've moved itself while they'd eaten. "I've got tonight off. Let's go meet your uncle."

* * * * *

Mirabelle had another, more compelling reason to visit her uncle that evening. With all the commotion of the previous night, no one had eaten the dinner that had spent hours simmering in Dutch ovens. Jameson had texted her with pictures of the food, telling her to come on over. At the lunch with Adrien, she'd been too flummoxed by his flattery to do more than nibble at the croissant sandwich, plus she craved real food.

Jameson and his wife, Mirabelle's maternal aunt, lived only a few blocks away from the café in an old gray stone home with green vines crawling up the chimney. Her grandparents had lived next door until they'd passed. Their home now belonged to Mirabelle's parents, who were currently on a year-long RV trip around the country. She'd gotten into the habit of going over to her aunt and uncle's at least one night a week for dinner—especially after her aunt's diagnosis.

"Just a heads-up," she said as they stopped in front of the house. "My aunt Isabelle has Alzheimer's. She can have stretches where she's fine, but then she makes a sudden swing to another time and place."

"I'm sorry."

She gripped the steering wheel. "Look, I know you think someone stole the ring, but go easy in there. You accost him in front of her, and I'll . . ."

He put up his hands. "I'll behave." His voice softened. "I promise. Plus, I'm more interested in what your uncle has to say about what he saw than accusing him of stealing."

Before they made it to the porch, her aunt threw open the front door and enveloped her in a hug. "Belle, darling. It's been weeks."

It hadn't. "Sorry, Aunt Isa, I've been so busy with work. I want you to meet my friend, Danny."

Isabelle immediately released Mirabelle and took in the new man. "Well, aren't you a tall drink of lemonade on a hot day." Her Southern accent always deepened around men. Not unlike Adrien, Isabelle always had a little flirt coming out. Even though Isabelle was seventy-five, Mirabelle swore half the men in town were in love with her aunt. Of course, she only had eyes for her husband.

"Danny, this is Isabelle, my most beautiful aunt."

Isabelle linked her arm through Mirabelle's and then caught Danny's and pulled him close. "Tell me how you met my darling niece and how you plan to win her over. Because, Danny, I am only telling you this once: she may be cheap, but she's not easy."

"Aunt Isa," Mirabelle sputtered, wishing she could melt into a puddle on the floor.

Danny had the audacity to laugh right out loud. "My plan was to paint her barn for her."

That "plan" stopped Mirabelle in her tracks. She'd been painting that barn for a year now and would probably need to start over by the time she finished.

"Oooh, I like that," Isabelle said. She winked at him. "I'll give you my blessing, but only if you actually paint the barn. All talk means nothing."

He had the smarts to nod quickly. "Yes, ma'am."

She abandoned them as soon as the door shut behind them to "see about dessert."

"Sorry," Danny whispered to her. "I thought with what you said, it would be easier to go along with things than try to correct her."

Much to her annoyance, he was right. Hopefully, he didn't keep up that habit.

Jameson came out of the kitchen to greet them, wiping his hands on a dishcloth. Mirabelle had texted him a heads-up about Danny and his suspicions. "Come sit down; dinner's almost warm, and y'all must be famished." Jameson spoke with a long drawl that had every word coming out like he'd carefully considered each one.

They sat around a large table on a braided rug in front of a fireplace. What Mirabelle's house had in chaos, this home matched in tranquility. Someday she hoped her home would feel like this—if that was even possible.

Isabelle allowed Danny to sit down but not do much more before launching into a series of questions about his past, present, and future. "A security guard at the festival, how fascinating." What Mirabelle loved about her aunt was her ability to make anyone feel comfortable and be completely invested in the smallest of stories.

"Not really," Danny said. "I was an FBI agent in New York, and that was fascinating."

"Why aren't you with them anymore?" She leaned forward in her seat, focusing entirely on him.

"I went after a criminal that had more money than I had proof, but I wouldn't let it go. I kept digging, upsetting some powerful people."

"You sound like a good man looking out for justice."

He stared down at the plate. "Maybe, but I couldn't prove it, and I couldn't let it go," he mumbled. As if remembering where he was, he glanced back up at Mirabelle. "I won't make that mistake again."

A load of dread filled her gut at having no idea who she'd let into her life. What if he couldn't let this go?

Jameson came around the table with a giant bowl of cheesy potatoes and dished them out. "Isa, let the poor boy eat."

With chicken, potatoes, biscuits, and green beans with bacon filling their plates, the first part of the afternoon was spent chewing in absolute delight.

Danny groaned only halfway through his plate. "I didn't know food could taste like this."

"Exactly," Mirabelle said. "Everybody says they come on the ride the first time for the ambiance; they come back the second and the third for the food. I don't know what I'll do when Uncle Jameson retires."

Truth was Jameson had already started doing less, with him not being able to leave Isabelle more and more. Mirabelle would make do, but it wouldn't be easy.

As if reading her thought, Jameson said, "Girl, I'm not retiring until I'm a hundred."

"You know," Mirabelle said to Danny, "Aunt Isa is my inspiration for the romantic rides. She took Uncle Jameson up on that ridge when they were dating to see the sunsets."

"Yes, to see the sunsets." Isabelle winked at Jameson. "It inspired our romance; why shouldn't it inspire others?"

Once everyone leaned back in their chairs with their belts loosened, Isabelle stood up and grabbed some dishes.

"I'll get them later, darling," Jameson said.

"No, you won't. I can't do the cooking justice, but I can clean a plate."

Usually, Mirabelle would jump up to help, but this would give them the opportunity to talk about the night without adding worry to her aunt's list of problems.

Danny must've realized the same thing. He immediately scooted his chair closer to Jameson. "Mirabelle said you would've seen more about what happened that night than anyone."

"I'm not sure how much help I can offer; I was prepping the food. Plus, they lost the ring a little bit up from the fire pit, so I didn't hear much until that woman started to scream like a bear had grabbed her."

"Did you talk to her at all?"

"Bethany? No, she didn't say one word to me. Could've well been invisible."

"But you were around the other couples? Anyone seem off or even different than usual?"

"Tamyra and her husband were in high spirits. That's Mirabelle's childhood friend. They were both all twitterpated about the pregnancy."

Mirabelle slapped her forehead. "I forgot they announced it. I need to call her; I am the worst friend."

"She'll understand," Jameson said.

Tamyra would, but that didn't excuse Mirabelle's forgetfulness.

"I bet Bethany wasn't happy with anything pulling the attention off her," Danny said.

Mirabelle laughed at his accurate assessment of a woman whom he'd never met. "Tamyra told the group before they arrived. She would've waited, but she was concerned she'd have to dismount to throw up and didn't want anyone to worry." She shook her head. "If Bethany had known that, she probably would've banned them from the evening."

"And the others?"

"Allie brought her fiancé," Jameson continued. "She was oohing and aahing over Bethany's ring."

Danny scribbled on his paper.

"Allie laughed when they compared the stones from her ring and Bethany's."

"I think Allie did that more for show than actual admiration," Mirabelle interjected. "It's not like her to be jealous or anything."

Danny turned to her. "The more you jump in to defend them, the more I want to question them. Makes it seem like you're overly worried I'll find something."

"That's not . . . I just don't." The more she sputtered, the more it did sound like she was trying to protect them. "Fine, you'll figure out for yourself how preposterous it is that anyone that night would steal."

"I have to agree with Mirabelle," Jameson said. "Plus, if I remember right, everyone was sitting around the campfire waiting for dinner when the ring went missing."

"Let's hope you're right," Danny said.

A deep chill filled the evening by the time Mirabelle walked Danny out and down the sidewalk. It would be an early winter. "Sure I can't give you a ride?" she asked.

"No, the sheriff lives a few blocks away. I've been staying with him." He pulled the collar up on his leather jacket and turned away.

"Danny," she said. "How come you're so sure?"

He paused in the lowering sunlight and seemed to take her question seriously. "Honestly, I don't want to be right. If one of your friends took it, I'm going to find it, because that's what I do. And when I do, it will destroy their life. I like solving crimes, but I don't like hurting people."

The heaviness of that weighed on her, and she said a quick prayer that he was wrong. She'd rather lose her company than destroy a loved one's life.

"But I can't let go of the feeling someone took it," he said. "Do you want me to stop looking?" He spoke with a sincerity that caught her off guard.

She seriously considered that for a moment. Doing so would mean losing everything, but . . . "No, I have faith in them." Would he have stopped looking if she'd asked him to? She doubted it, which was why she said no. But she did want to believe him when he said he didn't relish the consequences. If so, this was a man who did the right thing even when it hurt. And as mad as he made her, she had to respect that. "My friend Tamyra refuses to get up before nine, but I can see if we can come over after that."

"I'll pick you up this time."

Mirabelle about blurted out, "It's a date." Luckily, embarrassment flooded her, and she shut her mouth before she could. Where had that come from? "No, I'll pick up you up."

Without risking another word, she turned and fled to her truck.

8

The first thing on Danny's mind Wednesday morning when he woke up was the last thing on it when he'd gone to sleep—Mirabelle. Not so much her, obviously, but the ring. What would happen to her if he couldn't find it? What if Bethany, this woman he still hadn't met, decided to accuse Mirabelle of stealing it? He'd hate to see her pay for someone else's carelessness or greed—not if there was something he could do about it.

Danny had been honest when he'd told Mirabelle that he didn't want it to be anyone she knew, but they didn't have a whole lot of suspects to go with. She might not be willing to sacrifice a friend to save her company, but he would be.

He crawled out of bed into the fall chill of the morning, grateful for the thick rug covering the wood floors. Chris had been kind enough—or at least desperate enough for help—to put him up during the month of the festival. After that . . . Truth was, he didn't know for sure what after that would look like.

The man he'd pursued at the cost of everything had used his formidable power and connections to permanently end Danny's career at the FBI. Despite giving everything to his government, he'd been given two choices: quit or be fired. He'd almost gone with fired. Quitting went against every natural part of him. Luckily, the parts of him with common sense hadn't torpedoed his chance at a new career in a new field.

From the time he was a kid, he'd wanted nothing so much as to be a cop carrying more than a plastic badge. His father, a former Marine, ran things with a military precision Danny thrived under—especially in comparison to the rough neighborhood he grew up in.

Halfway through shaving, his phone dinged several times. He glanced down at the screen but didn't recognize the number. A swipe revealed both the sender and its message—Adrien had sent over more pictures of a ring than should ever exist.

He downloaded the files to his iPad and sorted them by timestamp. Not much changed between shots except a slight angle and the light. A quick scan proved they hadn't gotten the thief—either squirrel or human—in the shots. He swiped through them several times as something, he couldn't say what, didn't feel quite right.

His phone rang. "Hello."

"Are you ready?" Mirabelle's voice came through loud and clear. "I didn't wake you, did I?"

He glanced down at the towel he still wore and half his whiskers unshaven. "Can you give me thirty minutes?"

"A half hour?"

Did he detect a hint of judgment? He had a feeling Mirabelle did more by nine a.m. than most folks accomplished in a week. He'd never been a morning person, despite his father's best efforts. He was a "work all night" kind of guy. "That mess with your schedule?"

"No, it'll be fine. I can get the chicken coop cleaned out." They weren't that much different in one respect—it seemed neither one of them lingered when there was work to be done.

He wasn't entirely sure what cleaning out a chicken coop entailed, but he was entirely sure he didn't want to be stuck in a truck with her afterwards. "I'll be ready in ten minutes."

He rinsed off the last of the shaving cream as she honked for him outside. She'd allowed him an extra five minutes, but he still had to tie his shoes in the truck.

"Did you see Adrien's photos?" She pulled out into the road.

"Yes. Did he send them to you?"

"No, I was with him this morning."

Danny stiffened. "What for?" His tone rendered a judgment he didn't quite understand. What was it to him if they'd spent the morning together? He just hated to see any woman fall for a player's lines. Something about Mirabelle gave out a *naïve about men* vibe. *None of your business,* he reminded himself.

Mirabelle saved a glare from the traffic and used it on him. "You still think he's a suspect?"

As of matter of fact, he didn't, but Danny didn't know how else to explain his reaction. He just didn't like the idea of her being taken advantage of. "I'm not ruling anyone out."

"He was actually helping me look for the ring. I managed to borrow a metal detector and wanted to go over the area."

He didn't have to ask if they'd discovered something. If they had, they wouldn't be driving to meet another couple. "Is he still spreading the charm?" He cringed at his own stupid question, which was none of his business. Why couldn't he just shut up?

She blushed, and that didn't do his mindset any good. "Oh, it was quite thick this morning." She rolled her eyes. "He insisted on taking my photo. I don't much like it, but if I can dig myself out of this hole, the photos could be good for Instagram."

He hoped she'd keep her head on her shoulders and not fall for the French lover's flattery. However, as much as it pained him, he did have to agree with Adrien's assessment that Mirabelle's bright, beaming smile would be good for business. That is, if she bestowed it in the photos. One day with her and he'd only spotted the elusive smile when she was with her aunt or talking about her business. He wondered if he would be granted it today; then he wondered why it mattered.

"I texted Tamyra before I picked you up. She's waiting for us."

"How long have you known her?"

"Thirty-one years."

"You keep very good track."

She laughed, and he liked knowing he could cause another response besides anger. "Our mothers shared the same labor room at the hospital. Tamyra came first; I came second. Not much has changed. And no, I don't think she stole the ring, nor her husband."

He swallowed an argument. "Tell me all the reasons why they would."

Mirabelle opened her mouth ready with a retort, but to a different question. "Wait, what?"

He shrugged. "Once you see the reasons they would steal the ring, it's easy to see the reasons they wouldn't. Trust me."

She side-eyed him with a look that said she would do anything but. "Okay," she said hesitantly. "It's worth a lot of money."

"That's a reason for everyone. What are reasons specific to them?"

She gave it more thought. "Tamyra's impulsive. She does, and then she thinks. It's why we get along so well." She smiled at a memory he couldn't see. "For our eighteenth birthday, she took me for ice cream . . . in Philly. We wound up staying two days in the clothes we wore. Our parents were so mad."

"Her husband, Ty, is the exact opposite, though, which is what I guess would be his motive. She plays; he plans. I know having a baby will have him stressed about the money, the time, all the unknowns. That much money would get their kid into Harvard, which I'm sure he's already planning for."

Mirabelle spoke with a fondness for her friends that brought out a sense of longing in Danny. His adulthood hadn't lent itself to long relationships. Chris was his last friend in Brooklyn, but he'd left for a more affordable home for his growing family—like almost everyone else they'd grown up with. Their small town in the city had been swallowed up by the hipsters with more money. He felt a flash of pity for Mirabelle; her town was on the brink of the same thing. He hoped the big money wouldn't force her out of her home like it had done for him.

"Okay," Danny said. "Now why wouldn't they?"

"Right before our trip to Philly, Tamyra's grandmother had given her a credit card for emergencies. We were scrounging dollar bills in our purses for bus fare home—our parents were far too mad to help—but she wouldn't touch the card. I begged her to get us some cash. 'It's our choice; we pay,' was all she'd say."

"And Ty?"

"That man would pass out before he could even pick up the ring. He once got charged for one meal but bought two while we were all out at this restaurant. We were playing cards at their house later that night before he figured it out. I've never seen a man more on edge. He was outside the restaurant waiting the next morning for them to open. Even took off work. Does that satisfy your curiosity?"

It did to a certain degree. Her willingness to even think for a second that they might've done it actually worked in their favor. It was his experience that those who protested the most vehemently, who swore up and down their loved ones would and could never, either knew they had or deep down inside suspected they did.

Tamyra and Ty lived in a cottage with a walk covered in fall leaves. Pansies lined the path to the front door—not yet relinquished into fall. A few jack-o'-lanterns bookended the steps to the porch.

Before they could knock, Tamyra, he assumed, opened the door with a wide smile. Her black braids were pulled into a red bandana matching a bright apron tied tight over her small protruding stomach. Danny wouldn't have spotted the latter without knowing the big news they'd recently shared.

Mirabelle passed him and reached out with a hug. "Thanks so much. I know y'all are busy."

"No problem; this is important." Tamyra shivered a bit. "Come on in from the chill. I know they say babies are their own personal heaters, but that stage has not kicked in for me yet."

Danny followed the women into the kitchen but stopped in his shoes at the sight that greeted him. Stacks of boxes filled with pies—at least five each—covered almost every empty space other than one where a dough ball sat ready to be rolled out.

Tamyra must've caught his expression. "I know; it's something, isn't it? My husband, Ty, says next festival he's moving into a hotel for the month."

Clarity flowed through Danny. Everything in this town shut down and revolved around the festival for the entirety of October. "You're a baker?"

"Heavens, no," she blurted out. "But my mother is, and since she pushed me out of the womb, once a year I have to pretend to be. She mixes the dough and filling; I just assemble." She rubbed her belly. "I wonder what fun things I'll torture this one with."

"Whatever it is, I'm taking the baby's side against you every time," Mirabelle declared.

Tamyra stuck out her tongue. "I am your best friend."

"And *I* will be that baby's favorite aunt no matter the cost."

He understood why Mirabelle was confident in her friends. How could you not be for people you've known before you could speak?

Tamyra led them to the adjacent dining room where one side of the table remained clear. "Pick your poison," she said.

Before Danny could ask what she meant, Mirabelle jumped in. "Blueberry. No, apple. Wait, do you have ice cream?"

"There's no room left in the freezer for that." A deep voice came from the hallway, and Danny turned.

If he'd been playing a game of match, he would've never put Ty and Tamyra together. Ty wore a crisp plaid shirt with actual pens stuck in the pocket. His glasses would've been labeled thick ten prescriptions ago. He took the room in a few steps and reached up and kissed his wife on the cheek—reached up because he was a few inches shorter than her. Other than that, he kept his gaze mostly on the ground even when introduced to Danny.

Tamyra and Ty went to get pies—chocolate and banana cream because of the "no ice cream" situation.

"Don't worry," Mirabelle whispered. "He's not guilty, just really, really shy."

Two pieces later of the best pie he'd ever had, Danny leaned back in his chair worried he would burst. "This is amazing, thank you."

"And you only owe Tamyra twenty dollars," Mirabelle said. "Do you have the cash on you, or were you planning on stealing it?"

Danny sat straight up. "No, of course not. I don't have cash on me, but I'll . . ."

Tamyra shot him a stern look. "Figures. You New Yorkers think everything is yours."

He reached for his wallet to count what he did have, but out of the corner of his eye he spotted Ty shaking his head, and then Tamyra laughed. He turned to Mirabelle, who smirked at him. "Sorry, but with how serious you take things, you kind of had it coming."

As a peace offering, Tamyra went to get him another slice to take home while Mirabelle explained their visit. "Danny is helping me find the ring. He thought it would be good to talk to everyone and see what they remember."

"You don't think anyone could've stolen it, do you?" Tamyra asked.

"It seems the most plausible explanation to me," Ty spoke out. "I can't imagine it disappearing in such a short time."

All three heads turned to him. Only the two women replied. "How can you say that?" Tamyra said. "That would mean it was someone we knew."

Mirabelle jumped in. "Who could do such a thing?"

Ty looked to Danny as if pleading for a rescue. Danny wasn't one to acquiesce. First, he wanted to see the situation play out without his interruption. Second, he really didn't want to go up against both women. He'd only a recently established a truce with Mirabelle and could sense Tamyra wasn't someone to oppose.

Even without Danny's backup, Ty surprisingly held his ground with one concession. "That trail is a popular one; perhaps someone hiking saw the ring and took advantage of everyone being distracted. We saw people on the way up."

Both women took a moment while Danny sat back in his chair and pondered that.

"If that's the case," Mirabelle said, "then I'm in big trouble. How could we ever find it?"

"How long before the ring was stolen did you see other people on the trail?" Danny asked.

Ty looked to his wife for help.

"It was before the proposal," Tamyra said slowly, giving the answer some thought. "I remember a couple stopping to let the horses pass not far from the ridge."

"And another," Ty added, "around the same time. I remember because they commented on the smell of dinner and said they wished they were us."

Mirabelle stared at the half-eaten chocolate pie sitting in front of her, her face a study in discouragement. He didn't need to ask to know what thoughts flowed through her mind. If the ring had been lost, there was a chance she could find it. If it had been stolen by strangers, what could she do?

Danny answered the unspoken question. "There's plenty we can do. We can take their descriptions, maybe get a list of cars at the trailhead. Someone would've seen them."

She looked at him hopelessly. "In a week?" She paused. "Oh, wait, five days?"

"I'll talk to this Bethany. Maybe, if she knows we're making progress, she won't take it out on you."

"Sweetie," Tamyra said to Mirabelle. "This one woman can't destroy everything."

"You don't understand. The social media hoards can destroy a business or a reputation in twenty-four hours. It doesn't have to be true or even accurate. I can build it back up under a new name, but by that time I'll be worse than broke. She has millions of followers; I have no one."

Mirabelle was right. He'd seen lives destroyed by innuendo. Social media added fuel to the fire.

"So, we find the ring," Danny said simply, surprised by his words. He'd learned a long time ago to never promise a victim anything. Except he wasn't an agent anymore, and Mirabelle wasn't anyone's victim.

Tamyra had to get to the festival, hastening their departure. He'd asked a few more questions about the day but didn't press them too hard. These first visits were a fact-finding juncture more than anything. To get a clear picture of that night, he needed everyone's memories. Then he could start sorting the truths from the lies.

They climbed back into the truck. "Do you think they did it?" Mirabelle asked, half sarcastically, half serious. He knew she didn't believe in their possible guilt any more than she had that morning; she wanted to know his beliefs.

"No," he said without thinking his answer through. What was it about this woman that kept him blurting out things he shouldn't? "At least, it's doubtful, but they brought up a good point about there being others. Did you notice anyone hanging around?"

"No, but again, I was focused on making sure everything went smoothly."

"This isn't your fault." There he went again. "You can't control every outcome."

She laughed without mirth. "You know, my biggest fear about that day was the weather. We had a storm roll in that morning, and I was terrified it would linger."

"I remember that. It knocked out power down at the park, and we had to start the backup generators. This one woman—she had to be eighty—actually started an argument with me over the noise. She said I was ruining the experience."

"Was she wearing red?"

"Yeah, why?"

"You're lucky she didn't hit you. That's Mrs. Lindgren; her husband was mayor for a hot minute in the nineties."

"So?"

"Exactly. Nobody cares, but she thinks she runs the town." She shook her head with a smile. "She's the reason her husband's term in office lasted so little. Though, if she's the one to tell it, he got pushed out because the council was jealous of his popularity."

He considered his options. "Do I ban her from the festival, or do I avoid her?"

"You run like crazy. She got in a fistfight with the sheriff back then. That's what finally brought everything to a head. Life is too short."

Danny couldn't help but laugh at her dry tone until she joined in, her hair bouncing out of the elastic, which failed at its one job. When she smiled, the air around her changed. It almost buzzed. "Out of the two gray-haired women I've met in the last few days, I think I prefer Isabelle."

"Oh, you be careful," Mirabelle said, still smiling. "She won't start a fight, but she can cut a man down with a look."

"Is that why they named you after her?"

"No, they—" She turned in the truck seat and cut him down with a look. "What exactly are you implying?"

He leaned back under her gaze, before he caught a hint of an upturn in the corner of her mouth. What did Sherlock say? *The game was afoot.* "Nothing really. I just noticed your similar names and made a connection."

"Oh." She looked a little disappointed with his answer and went to put the key in the ignition.

"Oh, and your ability to freeze a person's soul with a stare like Medusa."

She returned the glare to him, but it had lost all its fierceness and instead held a bit of a sparkle. "Then you'd better be careful."

As much as he liked making her laugh, this was way more fun.

ad Mirabelle been flirting with a man? No, she decided, especially not that man.

His judgmental eyes on all her loved ones and on her did not allow her to even consider the idea of flirting with him. She'd been friendly to keep him on her side; that was all.

Her phone rang right as Danny climbed out of the truck at the festival where he had to report to work. Adrien's name flashed on the screen. Now that was a man she could exist harmlessly with. He was no more interested in her than he'd be in Mrs. Lindgren. Okay, a little more interested. She'd give herself that much credit.

"Belle, are we still on for photographing the farm tonight?" Adrien's accent was so different from Danny's; Danny still carried New York in his speaking—a tone that made everything sound a little more aggressive.

She slapped her forehead. How could she have forgotten? They were going to create promotional materials, which she would hopefully still need. She considered postponing until she was sure she'd still have a company in a few weeks, but the fall colors were so fleeting. The higher elevations were already brown and ready for snow. "Of course, but I don't have to be in them, right?"

"Don't be silly. You'll be the centerpiece."

She drove home, wishing for the first time she had more than fifteen minutes to get ready.

A half hour later, Mirabelle stood in front of her closet staring at her clothes next to a disapproving Adrien. She'd thought Danny had looked down on her; Adrien took one look at her stained jeans and shook his head. "You have the right theme, but the wrong look." He fumbled through her clothes until he pulled out a red shirt, an old leather jacket, and a pair of jeans with frays in the thighs from brushing up against a barbed-wire fence. "Put these on." He left her in the room.

When she went back outside, he was rinsing off a pair of rubber boots she used to muck out the stalls. "Better," he said, looking her up.

She couldn't figure out what was so different from what she'd been wearing. "Now what?" she asked as if she were being booked into jail.

"Go get your cowboy hat that you were wearing the night of the trail ride."

With a sigh to rival a five-year-old's, she went back inside and grabbed the hat that she did not muck stalls in because it was too nice for that. Why couldn't he shoot the farm without her in it?

She slipped on the now-clean boots and found Adrien moving bales of hay from the barn in random piles that did not make sense. He took what felt like a hundred shots of her standing in different poses all over the farm. Even her favorite gelding, Argus, sighed during the last few photos.

"We don't have much time before we lose the light," Adrien said. "We'll do the wide shots tonight and the close-ups another day."

Another day! Mirabelle wanted to scream. It took everything she had to sit there while he pushed and prodded her into various poses.

He must've realized what a long day it had been, because he finally put the camera down. "Why don't you walk around doing your normal evening work, and I'll follow you?"

Relief flowed through her so suddenly, she about sank to her knees. She fed, she shoveled, and she did her darnedest to avoid the camera, with zero success.

Adrien set the camera aside and reached into a stall to pat one of the horses while the animal ate and she filled a wheelbarrow. "Why do you hide every time I try to take a picture?"

"I don't," she said, a little defensively. "You've got a lot of shots of me."

"I have shots of you standing behind a pitchfork, ducking behind a door, and the classic turning away from the camera."

She didn't make eye contact as she continued throwing the green manure in. "I don't think I need to be in it."

"You really don't understand, do you?"

"I guess not."

"You, Mirabelle, are the face and the voice of the brand. People don't connect with a pretty picture; they connect with a person."

"I don't want to be a pretty person or a brand."

"If you don't get this right, it won't matter what Bethany says about you online. You need to become a personality people want to support, want to meet, and want to be like. Your brand is your story, and you can't be invisible." Adrien grabbed his gear. "Give it some thought."

Mirabelle didn't have to. She wasn't Bethany, thank you very much. She'd seen how the internet treated people and how it changed them, and she wanted no part of that. The Bethanys of the world had two personas—she'd stick to one.

In high school and then college, she'd watched girls change themselves over and over, usually for a boy. Even gorgeous Tamyra would switch her personality around, not to win over the boys, but to keep them at a safe distance until she figured out what they wanted. She'd had enough experience in high school with the super-nice guys who doted on her changing to jerks once she rejected them or dated them.

Mirabelle had observed all this from a safe emotional distance. Nobody noticed the freckled, flat-chested tomboy next to the tall goddess. And the few who did notice her only used her as a bridge to walk over to get to her best friend.

That was one of the reasons Mirabelle liked Ty so much; he hadn't treated her any differently than he had anyone else. Ironically enough, that was also why Tamyra fell hard so for him. Egghead that he was, he was oblivious to her beyond the accounting reports she provided his department. He complimented her on their accuracy and timeliness, barely noticing the woman behind them.

They'd all worked together at the same firm. Unlike Mirabelle, Tamyra had loved corporate life and numbers and spreadsheets. Mirabelle wouldn't have thought two people could fall in love over Excel, but Tamyra and Ty did. Once they'd gotten married, they'd moved back to Harvest Ranch, where Tamyra got a job for the town as an auditor while Ty commuted to Richmond. All in anticipation of children that, for many years, hadn't come until now.

It wasn't long after Ty and Tamyra had gotten married that Mirabelle had found herself falling for someone in the same building where they worked. She'd fallen in love with Eric quickly and completely—until he'd slipped the ring on her finger and started telling her all the plans he had for their life. A life that he hadn't—not once—asked her opinion on. Mirabelle giving up her life for his seemed to be the gist of their future.

For the first time, Mirabelle had realized that giving in to love meant giving up your independence. Even Tamyra had sacrificed her beloved career for family. Maybe others could be happy doing that, but not her. She looked back on that relationship in terror—realizing how close she'd come to losing herself.

That was why she had to be so careful around Danny and every single guy like him.

That night, just as Mirabelle's head finally hit the pillow, Tamyra shot her a text. *I like him.*

Mirabelle was far too tired and grumpy from having a camera in her face to play games about who and why. *Not happening.*

Winky-face emoji.

She slapped her phone face down on the nightstand next to a stack of books telling her how to successfully run her own business. After a deep breath, she lay down and closed her eyes.

Ding. She sat straight up and grabbed the phone so hard she ripped the charger out of the socket, determined to tell her friend what she thought about her opinions.

I think he likes you.

That brought Mirabelle up short. Tamyra was *not* one of those best friends who told you what you wanted to hear. She was the friend who said yes, that dress did make you look fat, but the other one was gorgeous on you.

Mirabelle punched her friend's name into the phone.

Tamyra answered on the first ring. "I'm not wrong."

"You are so wrong. The only time he thinks about me is to criticize."

"What has he criticized?"

"Only everything. My appearance, my yard, *my barn*." She listed the most important item last.

"Well, if that's the case, then he's a huge tool, and I will smack him the next time I see him, but maybe . . ."

"Maybe what?"

"What exactly did he say about your appearance?"

"That I smelled!"

Of all the responses a girl should get from her best friend in solidarity, hearty laughter was not one of them.

"Tam!"

"What? You do sometimes."

"But it's impolite to point it out."

"Did he say it in so many words?"

"He asked if I wanted to take a shower before we went to lunch, and then he stared at my pants."

"Did they have manure on them?"

Mirabelle didn't answer.

"Did they?"

"It doesn't matter."

"Okay, I'm giving him a point for that. What did he say about your yard?"

"Not in so many words, but when I came out *after showering*, he'd raked some leaves and cleaned it up."

"Mirabelle! If Ty cleaned up our yard without me having to tell him, the things I would do to that man . . ."

Mirabelle blushed all the way to her fingers. "My point is, he doesn't like me."

"He's helping without pay."

"He's sure one of us stole the ring."

"I can understand why he'd think that, but one of us didn't. And he looks at you when you're not paying attention."

"No, he doesn't."

"How would you know if you're not paying attention? Plus, you like him too."

Hanging up a cell phone did not have the satisfaction of what slamming a phone would have had. Maybe if she'd had that option, she wouldn't have allowed such nonsense. "Why? Because I say I don't like him. That's such a stupid cliché. The girl says she doesn't like him, so she must be secretly in love with him," she said in a high-pitched voice.

"No, because you're on edge around him. Honey, you're only uncomfortable around guys you like."

"No, I'm just waiting for him to put the handcuffs on. Plus, I like Ty and I'm comfortable around him."

"That's different and you know it. But this guy . . ." Tamyra continued. "You were even teasing him a bit about paying for the pies, and you don't tease men—you find fools."

She ignored that. "Why are you telling me this?"

"To tell you to get out of your head and enjoy whatever it is for however long it lasts. Don't overthink it, question it, or poke it until it's dead."

"Do I do that?" she asked quietly.

"You're so scared of repeating the past, you take every potential relationship apart to see how it works. The problem is, you can't put them back together again."

Mirabelle lost all her power to argue.

"Think of this guy as having a good time," Tamyra said. "He said he's not staying in town, so you know there's nothing long-term going to happen. Just enjoy his company, make him buy you a nice dinner, and if things get a little physical—"

"Tamyra!" Inability to slam or not, Mirabelle hung up the phone and went to bed—just not to sleep for a very long time.

10

anny sensed something had changed about Mirabelle. While the day before she'd been scattered, today she was downright skittish. Had she learned something about her friends she didn't want him to know?

He'd picked her up to visit the second couple from the proposal night. When he'd reached ahead of her to open his car door, she leapt a foot back. Then, when he'd asked her how her evening had gone, she sputtered, "Nothing happened, nothing at all. I mean, Adrien came over last night to take pictures, but that was it."

His hand gripped the gearshift as he remembered her plans for the prior evening. He'd forgotten, because she'd said it was all about business and she could see through his flattery. So much for that. Spending the evening with Adrien would explain her change in personality. He'd figured her for a woman who didn't get easily sucked into promises and lies—that she was smarter than that. Except maybe she was that smart and didn't care that Adrien was only interested in the here and now. But what was wrong with that?

They pulled up to their destination, and he threw the gear into park, jamming the brake into the floor. Nothing was wrong with it. It was none of his business. He jabbed the unlock button, then remembered he knew nothing about the next couple. While Mirabelle had spoken at length about Tamyra and Ty, she hadn't said much about these two.

His distraction at Adrien had kept him from noticing exactly where they'd driven to until he went to open the door. A massive white house surrounded by acres of farmland basked in the golden glows of the morning. A giant red barn in the back looked straight out of an autumn calendar.

He stole a glimpse of Mirabelle, who looked with longing at the barn. "Is that the dream?" he asked.

She sighed. "That's the fantasy. The dream is closer to my budget."

"Who are we seeing again?" he asked, making a note to look them up in more detail later. He should've done it the night before, but a fight amongst a few drunks who'd wound up having to be booked in jail had kept him at the festival until late. But whoever lived here didn't seem to need to steal a diamond.

"Allie and her fiancé, Tony. Allie and I have been friends since high school, along with her sister Jo and Tamyra. I don't know Tony very well; he's from elsewhere."

"Elsewhere?"

She shrugged. "He says he's from Portugal, but his accent tends to come and go depending on how charming he's trying to be."

"Why would Allie steal the ring?"

"She wouldn't," she hastily added, but then she caught his look. "Oh, right." She rolled her eyes. "Allie's father lost a lot of money to a crooked investor who took in a lot of folks in town. This beautiful home that has been in their family for generations just sold. As far as I know, their business is fine, but that money would probably bring them even with the bank, plus some."

Interesting. He took a mental note of that. "And why wouldn't she?"

"I've never met anyone who cares less about money than her. She's been super successful, but more out of ambition at growing her company. She'd see stealing like cheating at a board game. What's the point of winning if you can't do it honestly?"

"What about Tony?"

Mirabelle shifted uncomfortably in her seat. "I don't really know enough about him to say either way." Her saying nothing was saying something.

"When are they getting married? Are you stuck being bridesmaid?" He wanted to keep her defenses down.

Her face relaxed a little. "Next spring, and yes, I'll have to wear a bridesmaid dress." Her face screwed up in dread.

Danny laughed at the expression. "It can't be that bad."

"It's going to be pink and frilly; it will be that bad."

"Okay, you win." He paused for a second to let her relax a little more. "You must be pretty excited for them."

"Yep."

That "yep" said a lot in one word. Small problem was he couldn't exactly interpret it. If he was a betting man, it translated into, "I don't like this guy, but my friend is going to marry him, and there's nothing I can do about it."

"I supposed we ought to go in," he said, curious to see how she'd interact with them.

Allie answered the knock before they could rap a second time. Going by the smells in the house, they would be gifted to another amazing treat. No investigation had ever fed him so well.

"Come on in," the woman said, her red ponytail falling out and spilling everywhere. "Welcome to chaos." Apparently, no home in Harvest Ranch had any sort of order during the month of October.

Introductions were to Allie were made, and for the third time in three days, he was checked over in enough detail they could draw him from memory.

"No luck on the ring, I take it?" Allie asked.

"No, we're starting to worry—"

Danny reached out and touched the small of Mirabelle's back. Her back arched at his unexpected touch. "What is that amazing smell?" he asked.

"Honey wheat bread. I like to have a few baked goods to attract people to our booth. Do you want a slice?"

"Yes, please."

She slipped back to the kitchen.

Without realizing he did it, Danny's hand flattened to rest on Mirabelle's back. She leaned closer ever so slightly, her warmth seeping into his hand. All thoughts of the ring momentarily fled, and he found himself without words. He hadn't stood this close to a woman in a long time.

"What's wrong?" she asked.

Absolutely nothing, he wanted to say, but then he found his thoughts again. Danny leaned in closer and whispered in her ear. "Don't say anything about the other hikers. I want to see what she noticed without any prompting."

Mirabelle nodded before glancing down.

He followed her gaze to where his hand still wound around her back. Without realizing it, he'd grasped her flannel shirt. "Sorry." He dropped the fabric.

"I've got the bread."

They both jumped back. Allie smiled a little smugly as she passed them to set the plate piled high with thick slices on the table.

Danny shook off the moment and smothered a thick slice in honey butter, taking a giant bite. He didn't swallow but savored, not believing he would ever taste anything that good again. How many more couples did they have to interview? At this rate, he hoped it was a few more. Once he'd taken another slice, he looked around. "Where's your fiancé?"

"Oh," Allie said breezily. "He couldn't make it. Our company, Sticky and Sweet, is growing so fast we've got investors coming in, and he has a lot to do before that."

Mirabelle sat next to Danny but out of his sight as he faced Allie on the other side. Despite that, he could've sworn he heard her eyes roll.

"I'd still like to talk to him," he said.

"We were together. Anything he saw, I saw." She spoke with a perky voice, but Danny spotted something in her eyes. Was it fear? Disappointment?

He would find this Tony, but right now he focused on her. "What did you see?"

"Honestly, nothing." She pulled the elastic from her ponytail and redid it. "Tony and I were talking about our own wedding and what we wanted. We were in our own little world."

Behind him, Mirabelle cleared her throat. "Was Tony all right? He seemed a bit . . . distracted."

Danny wondered what term she'd substituted out.

"Oh, yes," Allie added quickly. "He got there late. Some work stuff came up, and he was a little flustered. The business is growing rather quickly," she explained to Danny. "We're really excited, but it's been a lot of work for him."

He made a note to investigate this Tony. He still had some friends who could look him up. "Where were you when the ring went missing?" he asked.

"Let's see. I think I was talking to Jameson when I heard that woman scream." She turned to Mirabelle. "She can't blame you. I was talking to Tony about it, and he suggested you get a lawyer."

Mirabelle sighed. "I can't afford a lawyer."

"At least go talk to one for an hour. Get some advice. If she comes at you, you'll need to know what to do. We could even get a GoFundMe."

Mirabelle jumped to her feet. "No, I don't need to beg on the Internet. I can solve this."

With a yank on his sleeve, Danny followed her up, knowing enough not to argue.

"Sorry, Allie. I've got eight guests coming tonight, and I need to prep." She didn't stop all the way to Danny's car. He would've liked to have asked more questions, but he figured he could return now that introductions had been made and talk to Tony later.

He drove her home, the dust from the dirt road floating behind them. Washing a car was a waste of time in this neck of the woods.

"Danny," she said in a quiet voice. "Do I need to get a lawyer?"

He opened his mouth and tried to start a couple of different sentences, but nothing came out. He needed to tell her he couldn't promise to find the ring and maybe she should get a lawyer, but that didn't come out. He wanted to tell her she'd get through this, but he didn't know that for sure. "We'll find it."

She turned those soft brown eyes to Danny. "Really?"

What ended up coming out wasn't at all what he'd planned. "I've got the night off. What if I came tonight and got a feel for things? Maybe I'll see something that will give us an idea."

Why had he just offered that? After he dropped her off, he was supposed to drive the two or three hours to DC for an interview on a job for private security at a Fortune 100 company. He shouldn't cancel—not this late.

"Are you sure?" she asked. "I'd love you to see the night in action." She spoke with pride.

He needed to retract his statement, offer another day, but then she looked at him, pleasure brimming, and those words slipped away to be replaced by others. "Yeah, it's no problem." Pushing the interview back a week wasn't that bad of an idea. It was more a networking thing than an actual interview. And he hadn't felt this good about life in a long time.

"I'd sure appreciate it. Maybe you'll see how easy it would've been for someone to come without being noticed."

"Maybe." He really needed to be careful about his promises, but then she smiled. Danny really liked making Mirabelle promises.

11

Four couples wandered around the barn, snapping pictures of themselves in various poses with the horses and the hay bales. Mirabelle would need to thank Adrien for setting up the barn to be a fitting Instagram backdrop. That night they had a wide spectrum of couples, from one on a second date to one on a fiftieth anniversary.

She always provided dusters, chaps, and helmets—although that was more for liability—for anyone who wanted the full rustic experience. The women always leaned into it, but the men were hit and miss. That night two men egged each other on—much to her relief. The mood of the crowd could change on a dime. It always helped when a few of the guys could laugh and joke and be a little silly with it. That gave permission to the rest.

Danny hadn't showed up yet, and she jumped at the sound of every car on the gravel driveway. Then she berated herself for jumping at every car. She'd been on edge ever since that morning. Of all the times in her life when she didn't need a distraction, this ranked number one. Everything that mattered to her lay on the line.

But then he'd put his arm around her, and for a lingering moment, her world had felt completely at ease. Everything would work itself out; she'd known it in her bones. But like the mirage of a dehydrated person, that feeling couldn't be trusted.

As she adjusted the tack on a horse, Danny pulled up outside and stepped out of the car, wearing jeans and a plaid shirt and looking more handsome than she wanted to admit. It was the first time she'd spotted him without the uniform—and there was something about a man out of uniform.

She cringed at that errant thought that had no business rushing through her mind. She blamed Tamyra for it.

Tamyra. Maybe she was right; maybe Danny could be a safe way to practice dating at an emotionally safe distance. If she wasn't so dehydrated of male attention, the mirage would disappear. That was all the swirling emotions of the morning added up to—too many years alone.

She pulled down on the stirrup she'd been adjusting. "You're good to go," she said to the very tall man who would almost have to lift his feet to keep the stirrups from dragging. Despite his height advantage, he looked ill at ease at the entire endeavor. "The horse knows the way, I promise."

He nodded but didn't speak. She made a mental note to ride next to him the first little while.

With a smile that felt way too forced, she greeted Danny. "Welcome. You're just in time."

He came so close, she thought for a second he was coming in for a hug. She lifted her arms and then put them back down again. Then she lifted just one like she was going to pat him on the shoulder but dropped it. He took a step back before dropping his gaze.

Could that interaction have been anymore awkward? She really did need to practice. She could feel her cheeks betraying her as they so often did—but around this man in particular.

He leaned in. "Who's here that was also here the other night?" he asked quietly.

"No one. Even Uncle Jameson sent a friend Blake to help with the food. Aunt Isabelle had a bad day, and he didn't want to leave her."

"Who's Blake?"

She gestured to a young man loading supplies into a teal Ford truck from the sixties. "Jameson is sort of like an honorary uncle to him. Of course, he's that to most of the town."

"Wouldn't he need to be up by now cooking the food? I thought Dutch ovens take a while."

"They do, and he is." At Danny's confused look, she explained. "They get the food cooking and then drive back down to meet the guests. Every once in a while, I get a client who thinks they're ready to ride a horse but balk at the last minute. Jameson or Blake can drive them up, and then they hike up the last little bit to the ridge and meet the group."

"You've thought of everything, haven't you?" The FBI agent sounded downright impressed, and she swelled with pride.

"I'm always learning and improving."

"Well, then, I suppose I'd better sit back and enjoy the night. Which wild stallion is mine?"

Pleasure surged through her at the thought of an evening without the worry of the ring, doing what she did best. She pointed him in the direction of an already saddled gelding, who twitched an ear as Danny approached him.

That he had no interest in her, she was felt certain of. She could flirt at him without caring whether or not he reciprocated. And who knew? Maybe she'd soften him up a little and he'd believe her about her family and friends.

Mirabelle snorted so hard at the thought she startled the mare she was saddling, who snorted back in indignation.

She walked up to one couple who were arguing about the proper side to get on the horse. "It doesn't matter," said the man.

"We actually always mount from the left side," she offered with a smile, trying to be careful of the couple's dynamic. She noticed that when some men were put in unfamiliar situations, they acted overly confident and surly. "While either side gets you on, we want the horse to anticipate what's coming. Surprising these animals is always something to be avoided."

"See, I told you." the woman hissed.

"It's a good question," Mirabelle said, trying to placate the argument. Some of her "romantic" rides ended in fights. She'd learned enough about relationship dynamics in the last year to take on counseling as a second job when this one failed. *If,* she reminded herself.

Danny came up behind the couple. "This is my first time, too," he said. "I'm a little nervous about ending up on the upside down of the horse." He winked at Mirabelle, and she had to press her lips together to keep from smiling back. The warmth that shot through her, though, wouldn't be contained.

"You'll be fine," the husband said, turning to Danny with a scoffing tone, but he did relax a tad. "Although I'm looking forward to the dinner afterward."

Mirabelle left them talking to check on everyone else. As she slipped past Danny, she couldn't help but reach out and squeeze his elbow in thanks. She kind of wished he could come on more nights. She noticed he had a way with getting people to relax and start talking—even her, as much as she fought it. Then she remembered his reason for being around, and she didn't have trouble picturing him at being very good at getting a confession.

She mounted her horse, Argus—a bay who refused to follow another horse, hence why she took him. His eager hooves took the trail, always determined that this day would not be the one when others would pass him. They only had to ride for about four miles to get to the ridgeline, which allowed plenty of opportunity for Instagram moments along the way.

She kept them to the trail below the ridge until right before the sun reached its perfect coloring. That way, their first view would be jaw-dropping. She led them up the rocky trail, the horses slowly picking their paths. The sunset with its vibrant reds, oranges, and purples still caused a thrill. She nudged Argus off the trail into the trees and waited as each rider crested the pinnacle. Hearing the delighted gasps of her clients was her favorite part of each night.

This night, a few dark clouds cut through the sky, creating a border between the last of day and the beginning of night. By the time they would make their way down to dinner, stars would share the sky with the last vestiges of light. Everyone dismounted and tied off their horses.

Watching the couples line up for photos and planting kisses on each other always brought a stab of loneliness. During the summer, she broadened the groups to accommodate families, singles, and longer day trips. It was only during the festival that she advertised it as a romantic night and charged extra. Four weeks of extra money always brought four weeks of extra pain.

For the first part of her past relationship, she'd enjoyed the glorious adrenaline of being in love and loved. So bright was its glory, she hadn't noticed how his friends had priority over hers, and she'd been able to ignore the little jabs about how unrealistic her dream to buy a farm was.

Mirabelle hated that she still longed to have someone look at her the way these couples gazed upon each other. She envied the good-natured teasing, the quick pecks, and the longing looks; she even envied the short squabbles.

She'd built a life that people dreamed of, and she wouldn't trade that for the world. But sometimes she still longed for an everyday love. She stood and brushed the dirt off her chaps along with the thoughts in her mind. That kind of love required too big of a sacrifice.

The shadows crossed over the ridge, and she needed to mount up the group to head down the hundred or so feet to the campfire. The dinner bell would be ringing soon. Yes, Jameson or whoever always rang the triangle at dinnertime. Every detail had been accounted for.

The brush rustled behind her, and she turned to find Danny huffing his way up the trail. "Still not used to the elevation," he said before pausing for a deep breath.

"Where have you been?"

"I wanted to get a look down the other trail leading up from the parking lot, but it's already too dark under the trees." She led her groups up a side trail from her barn. It crossed several people's private property, which she had permission to cross but the public did not. "If someone outside the group stole the ring, they would've come up from there," Danny continued.

"What were you looking for?"

"Nothing specific. I wanted to get an idea on crowds, how far they'd have to go before getting to their car, that sort of thing. How's it going up here?"

"Just taking a second to enjoy the view. It's one of the perks of the job." And one she would miss so much if they failed.

He looked out as if noticing the skyline for the first time before disregarding it completely. "How long until dinner?" he asked.

So much for using this guy as practice. He didn't have a romantic bone in his body, which relaxed her now that she knew her heart wasn't at risk.

As if on cue, the triangle bell rang out. Everyone jumped to their feet and mounted their horses for the very short ride down.

While everyone filled plates with chicken and dumplings, she quietly unsaddled the horses and put the tack in the trailer driven up most nights by her neighbor's son—a sixteen-year-old who loved to hustle for extra gas money and the excuse to drive. She would drive two of the couples, and Blake would drive the others. That way no one had to ride back down in the darkness.

The sixteen-year-old, a gangly boy named André, stared over at the fire with a sigh after every stripped saddle he helped her with. She could read his hungry longing through the darkness, but she appreciated he didn't ask for food until the last horse had been brushed.

"So . . .?" he finally dared venture.

"Go," she said. "I promise they saved a plate for you."

He bounded off. She should follow, go mingle. If Jameson were here, she wouldn't bother. His easy charm and knowledge of the mountain history would enthrall the guests as the fired died down. This time of year, he'd probably have a ghost story or two to tell. The only ghost story she could think of was the mystery of the disappearing ring.

She approached the fire, and the voices carried over in the cool night air. "I just had to book an evening when I saw Bethany's post," one of the women said.

"I'm so glad you told me about it," said another.

Mirabelle stayed in the shadows, wanting the conversation to continue unfettered by her presence.

"Who's Bethany?" questioned one of the men.

"Oh, she's the best, and not like other influencers who fill their feed with just bikini shots and duck lips."

"Nothing wrong with a bikini shot," said, obviously, by one of the men.

"Though she's rich like some of the others," the woman continued, completely ignoring the man's joke, "she's totally self-made, and she's written these really good books on how to get over yourself and get what you really want. I've read all of them."

It was a good thing Mirabelle stayed in the darkness, as the rolling of her eyes almost pulled her to the ground. How did they know about Bethany's night? With no ring to flaunt, she hadn't posted anything. Mirabelle had been obsessively checking.

"Did she post about coming here?" Danny asked. "Is that how you found out about it?"

"She did a live story last week gushing about the view and the company."

"Can I see it?"

"Oh, no. Stories don't last. She's done several since then."

"When do you think she'll get engaged?" the other woman asked. "She was dropping a lot of hints in the last few weeks. I keep checking every day. I'm so excited for her."

That was what people didn't understand about Bethany's influence.

Here were two women who didn't even know her, completely invested in her life like she was their best friend. If Bethany said to buy something, they would. If she said to destroy someone, they would.

"Oh gosh, you're right. Even in that last video, she mentioned something about all the relationship advice the other couples were giving her, and how to make something worthwhile last for fifty years."

Part of Bethany's instructions to Mirabelle had been to gather happy couples she could video and use as advice for couples everywhere. "October is going to be the month of love," she'd said. "February is far too crowded. I want my fans to have greater love and connection throughout the year." Bethany toggled between mean girl and brand icon within conversations. "But make sure they photograph well."

By that time, Bethany's fiancé had already reached out to her to set up the proposal, and Mirabelle had been in too deep to cancel everything. *Just grit your teeth and get over it,* she'd told herself over and over. If only she'd canceled everything right then and there.

After cobbler, Mirabelle loaded all the horses and clients in the trucks and trailers and drove them down the ridge. The taillights of the last client disappeared out of her yard and into the darkness as she heaved a sigh of exhaustion. Before Bethany, these nights had been so fun, but now she waited for someone to blow up.

"Should I put the horses away?" Danny asked, startling her out of her dark thoughts.

She appreciated he didn't ask if he could help or dither around. "Yes, please." Her exhausted mind didn't allow for pride.

"How many horses do you have?" Danny said as he led a large black gelding to its stall—or the horse led him.

"I don't own them all." She closed the stall door behind her own horse and tossed over a pile of hay into a manger in the corner. "Some belong to neighbors and are older and not able to compete like they once were. The owners want to hold on to them out of sentimentality or the chance to ride once a week. They pay for feed, and I board them for free in exchange for using them on trial rides."

As soon as Danny closed the door, the black gelding shot its head over, forcing Danny to jump back. "He was all gentle and obedient on the ride," he muttered.

"Don't get in the way of his dinner." She threw a bunch a hay over, which the horse bit into and threw around before it could hit the manger. A spray of dried hay leaves coated both their heads.

Danny shook his head to free the particles. "Lesson learned. Did Jameson mention talking to Bethany?"

She didn't bother to shake her head. Those leaves weren't coming out of her curls without a good brush. "No, why?"

"Bethany mentioned in her video getting advice on how to stay married for fifty years, so I just assumed she had."

"No, but Bethany likes to exaggerate the truth."

"Yeah, most people do or play it down." The black horse, happy now that it had a mouthful of hay, threw its head over the door. Danny reached up and scratched under its chin.

"You've seen a lot of the dark in the world. Does that make it harder to trust?" she asked.

His hand paused for a minute before continuing to scratch. "No, but it does mean I see through the grays of a situation long before others would. Sometimes that makes it hard to form relationships, because I see all the reasons it could go wrong months and years before it does."

She moved to the other side of the gelding and made eye contact with Danny. "Do you ever jump in anyhow?" One of the reasons she enjoyed her work so well was she had an intense curiosity about people and their stories.

"I did—once. We were together just over a year, but I knew from the first date she would never be okay with my being an agent."

"But you still dated her?"

"It wasn't supposed to be long-term. She was about to take a job in London, but then that fell through and we kept dating. She swore it was fine, and I thought if I solved one more big case, I could move into a supervisory position to make my career more stable."

"What happened?"

The horse jerked his head back into the stall for another bite, and Danny quickly glanced down. "I got that last case, and I couldn't let it go. She realized I would always be a cop, and I realized I had seen through her lies to herself but not my own."

Mirabelle longed to have the right thing to say, but instead she went with her own curiosity. "Was it worth it? Staying as long as you did, knowing it was going to end?"

"No, because I spent too much time trying to be something I wasn't, and

I wasted her time thinking I was going to change." His sorrowful dark eyes found hers, and she found herself wanting to know his life story. "Maybe it would've been worth it, if I was honest from the get-go and so was she. That way we could've enjoyed what it was for as long as it was."

He grabbed his jacket off a nearby hay bale. "It's late. I should go."

She fought the letdown she felt and followed him to the barn door, where his car was parked just outside. "I tried for a while to be something I wasn't," she said. "I'm not afraid of losing the money; I'm afraid of going back to the lie."

He hesitated with his hand on the car door.

"What are you going to do if you can't be an agent?" she asked.

"I don't know." He offered her a sad smile. "I guess working as a security guard and helping a woman find a ring isn't a career solution, but it works for now." He slid in and started the engine.

Mirabelle wrapped her arms around herself in the cold night air. She knew something about working a job that paid the bills but did nothing for her. It'd sucked her soul dry and left her as a shell. The terror of going back to being that person meant she had to find that ring.

He backed up the car to turn around, and she reached back through the barn door to shut off the lights. As she walked to the house, he stopped and rolled down his window. "It didn't work, trying to be something you're not?"

"No, I came out anyhow."

"Thank you, Mirabelle. It's been an illuminating night."

She stood watching his taillights fade away. Maybe there wasn't a whole lot of romance in the man, but there was definitely something more solid and intriguing. And maybe a little practice flirting wouldn't be such a bad idea.

riday evening brought out the weekend crowds. Tourists had arrived
the night before, schools closed early for the day, and everyone
wanted to see the booths before it all shut down for the large dance
gearing up.

Danny wandered through the growing crowds with a constant eye.
There would be no taking time off today, no job interviews, no distractions,
and no Mirabelle. At least, that was what he told himself before she texted
him and he answered—twice. She'd created flyers and had spent the morning posting them around the festival with the help of one his guards.

Thinking about her got him thinking about his situation. He couldn't
be an agent anymore. What choice did he have besides going the private
route? He'd have better money and a stable schedule, and then maybe he
could have a relationship that would last longer the calendar year. But the
thought of doing that permanently just didn't sit right.

Out of the corner of his eye, he spotted a blonde girl eyeing up a bracelet while constantly looking around her. He caught her eye and winked.

She quickly put down the bracelet and disappeared into the crowd. A little thrill shot through him at the prevention of a crime. Maybe he'd scared her enough she wouldn't try again.

The crowds thinned as more and more people wandered over to the dance at the large town barn. As the festival had grown, so had the dance. It now spilled into an open field the town had cordoned off under the maples and dogwoods. Almost everyone made it to one of the weekly Friday dances—a lot made it to them all.

The moon rose in the eastern sky crawling its way over the hills. Tall heaters every fifteen feet or so gave off little flames, adding to the ambiance of the night and keeping the crowd warm between dances.

"Danny," a friendly voice called out.

He turned, not recognizing it. Beyond Chris and his family, he really didn't know anyone in this town who'd greet him like a friend.

"Danny, over here." The crowd broke up, and he spotted Tamyra waving at him from behind a stack of pies piled in boxes on a table.

It wouldn't hurt to take a few minutes and talk to the booth owners to get the skinny on things—and maybe a piece of pie if she were to offer it.

She greeted him with a grin like they were old friends and a piece of pie like they were best friends. "How's it coming with the ring?" She held back the plate, and he recognized a bribe when he saw it.

"I don't know. We hear something interesting, but then it doesn't pan out."

His deliberately vague answer must've been sufficient, because she passed over a chocolate piece doubled in height by whip cream. He took a bite and savored it.

"Tammy, girl." A woman walked up who had to be Tamyra's mother, going by the stern voice. "What are you doing giving away the product?" Her eyes turned to Danny. "Oh, I see. Buying off the law enforcement so they actually do their jobs."

His eyes widened, and the pie threatened to topple under the trembling fork. "No, ma'am. I know your . . ."

A hint of a smile played at her lips. He turned to Tamyra, who was trying but failing to hold in a grin by staring at the ground.

"You are a serious one; Mirabelle was right," the woman said.

"What did she say?" he blurted out, and he promptly turned his stare to the ground. Going by everyone's actions, the yellowing grass had to be the most fascinating thing at the festival.

After a good laugh, Tamyra saved him . . . a little. "Danny, this is my mother, Evelyn Murphy."

"But you call me Evie." Evie stood a good foot shorter than her daughter, but she had the same mocking smile. He would like to meet the dad. "I don't suppose it matters what Mirabelle thinks," Evie continued.

"It doesn't?"

"Does it?"

He cringed. One minute of conversation and this woman had already backed him into a corner. They could use her skills at the FBI. "I suppose not," he replied casually. It wasn't checkmate yet. "How are sales?"

She squinted at him and weighed her next move. "Good. Not as good as last year, though."

Ha! He'd won the game, but he felt an instant twinge of regret. He still didn't know what Mirabelle thought of him. No way Evie would pass on that information as long as he feigned disinterest.

Wait, why was he interested? He didn't need to care what that woman thought of him. As soon as he found the ring, he wouldn't see her again. Another twinge hit him, and this one he didn't have a name for. For the first time, he felt a little less gung-ho about solving a case.

While he ate the rest of his chocolate pie, Evie trailed off on a long list of previous festivals and each year's sales totals. She was probably hoping to bore him to death to get him to ask more questions.

It wasn't going to work.

"Is Mirabelle coming tonight?" Danny would return to his office, find the nearest roll of duct tape, and wrap it around his head until his mouth could no longer betray him.

"Once she finishes her ride," Tamyra said, not letting her mother turn his question into another round. "They're usually down by eight, and the dances go to midnight."

"Oh, good," he said rather lamely. "I wanted to ask her something about the ring."

"Jameson is over by the lemonade. He'd probably know, especially if he helped out tonight."

"Thanks."

Before he could take two steps, Evie slipped in one last zinger. "When you do see Mirabelle, try to convince her to dance, won't you? She hardly ever gets out there. Most of the men worth having in this town are already had." She changed her mocking grin to a sweet smile.

All he could do was admit defeat and nod his head. "Yes, ma'am."

It took him a bit to find Jameson. He had to stop three times to give directions, twice to stop people from littering, and once to help a missing little girl find her parents. By the time he made it over to the lemonade booth, Jameson had disappeared. He found him ten minutes later sitting next to a skinny pine tree on a folding chair by Isabelle, whose sparkling eyes never left the dancers.

Jameson climbed to his feet at the sight of Danny. "How's it going with everything? Mirabelle didn't have much of an update tonight."

"Did you go up the mountain with her?"

"Yeah, she'll be here soon. She wanted to change."

Danny glanced around but didn't see her. He hadn't figured she would take longer than Jameson to get ready.

"Danny," Jameson said. "Would you mind sitting with Isabelle while I go get us some drinks? I won't be but a few minutes."

He ought to protest, but he wanted the opportunity to talk to Isabelle on her own. Alzheimer's or no, he suspected she saw more of what was going on than anyone cared to admit. "Of course not."

Jameson hurried off, and Danny sank into his chair.

Isabelle gave him a confused smile. "I'm sorry, but have we met?"

"Yes, ma'am. I'm a friend of Mirabelle's." Seeing her embarrassed look, he quickly added, "But we just briefly met once."

Her eyes softened. "You're a beau of Mirabelle's?"

Surprised by the old Southern term, he stuttered a bit. "I'm not . . . we're not." Why was it every time he tried to question someone, he ended up with his back against the wall?

"The music is quite robust tonight. I'm not sure how long we'll stay." Isabelle politely steered the conversation out of the slide.

"Yes, it is," Danny said gratefully. "Did you go up the mountain tonight? That would wear me out too."

"Not tonight, no." Her words faded.

Danny wanted to tread very lightly to not upset her. "I went up there just yesterday. It was so beautiful."

"Yes, I suppose." In other people, her hesitation would read as lying, but he suspected it had more to do with not remembering and not wanting to admit the struggle. She straightened as some clarity seemed to break through. "It stormed this week. The lightning danced across the mountains like a ballet dancer."

The last time it stormed had been the morning of the infamous horse ride. "I'd never seen anything quite like it. The power was out for most of the morning, if I remember right."

Her face darkened—even in the shadow of night, he could see the change. "I didn't like it, and Jameson wasn't home. I couldn't find him." Tears welled in her eyes as she whirled around. "Where is he? Where's my JJ?"

So much for not upsetting her. "He's right there, see?" He pointed to where Jameson stood at a table waiting for sweet tea. "He'll be right back."

She leaned forward out of her chair to stand.

He needed something to distract her, not wanting her to wander away in this crowd. "I was thinking about asking Mirabelle to dance, but I'm worried she won't say yes," he blurted out. "What do you think I should do?"

She hesitated with her hands on the end of the armrests. "My Mirabelle?" she asked somewhat tentatively.

"Yes," he said, already regretting his choice in changing the subject. "It's okay; I don't suppose I'll ask her tonight."

Isabelle eyed him up with a look that shrank him down. "I suppose not in those plain clothes. A gentleman ought to dress up a little when pursuing a girl. My Jameson showed up in a tie to take me out for the first time for a burger."

His dad would probably have agreed with her. But somehow Danny didn't think Mirabelle would much care if a man showed up for a date in a tie. In fact, that would likely be points against him.

"There she is now. And will wonders never cease? She's gotten dressed up."

His head jerked up to spot Mirabelle standing at the edge of the crowd, perched next to the dance floor. Without Isabelle's callout, he would've never recognized her. The woman he knew did not look like that.

Her massive curls had piled up on her head, revealing her neck and collar where a necklace hung down. She wore an orange dress—something that he hadn't suspected she owned—that fell to above her knees and a pair of clean cowboy boots. All of it deeply unsettled him, and he couldn't say why.

Then he spotted the reason for the change and his unsettled feelings. Adrien stood at her side, talking into her ear, and she laughed. She didn't need to do all that to attract a man—especially a man such as that one. All she had to do was flash that mocking smile, and a man worth anything would accept the challenge.

Jameson spoke beside him, having returned with two drinks. "It's nice to see her looking like a woman for a change. I tell her men won't notice her otherwise."

Danny disagreed entirely with that statement, but he finally had the awareness not to broadcast it out loud. Unfortunately, that awareness did not extend from his mouth to his legs. Without realizing he'd made the decision to do so, Danny strode across the dance floor. He forgot about the ring, about his career, and about his current responsibility.

She caught sight of him a few feet away and straightened up, with Adrien taking a step back.

Danny held out his hand. "Dance?" Before her startled expression could come up with an answer, he took her hand and led her out on the dance floor while the band struck a slower tune.

They both stood there somewhat awkwardly. "You know," she said, "I was just telling Adrien that I can't dance."

He placed one hand on her waist and moved closer, almost touching her body with his, but not quite. "We'll give it a shot."

Her gaze left his and immediately went to her feet, where they shuffled back and forth. She wasn't kidding, but he didn't care. He didn't ask her to dance for skill reasons. The reasons why he did ask her were best ignored for now.

Figuring their best success would be in distracting her from the actual act of dancing, he tried to draw out a conversation. "I didn't mind last night, being up on the ridge at sunset."

She finally looked up, and he caught a close glimpse of her dark eyes. "You didn't seem to notice much beyond the investigation."

He flinched slightly. That had been his girlfriend's constant complaint against him. "I did notice. I've just gotten into the habit of not always communicating everything I observe." He hadn't realized how much of his work life had blended into his personal life. Had his holding back been the reason all his relationships had gone so wrong, or had they all been inevitable? "You made that night perfect down to every detail. I watched you time everything to the second while the guests were absolutely oblivious to everything but having a good time."

A smile spread across her face and reached her eyes. She didn't blush or glance away or act all fake modest. "Thank you," she said simply. "It's been a lot of work, but the results are worth it."

She had the same passion for her work as he did for his. He liked that she was so very straightforward. Her hand pressed against his back a little tighter, and they fell into a rhythm with minimal stepping on each other's toes. The heat off their bodies created a connection between them.

As the last strums on the guitar faded away, they broke apart, but something had changed between the two of them. For the first time, Danny sensed they were on the same side. He didn't want to let go, but then he remembered his responsibilities.

He took a breath. "I should get back to work," he said. "Never know what this crazy town might be up to. I have to walk the parameter of the lake and clear out all the teenagers who think they're invisible down there."

"Are there many?"

"A few, but they scatter pretty fast when I shine the flashlight on them."

"Would it be alright if I walked with you partway? I'd love to catch some shots of the harvest moon rising over the lake. Adrien has inspired me to take more photos showcasing the place."

Danny flinched at that man's name, which probably fed his response more than common sense did. "Sure. Most everyone is at the dance anyhow." Despite his almost forty years, he couldn't help but smirk at the Frenchman as they walked past him, his hand still at Mirabelle's waist.

13

The moon reflecting off the water made for a photographic sight that would garner a lot of likes. Mirabelle barely noticed any of that as the man who walked beside her took her elbow.

The drastic change in her appearance that night had been at Adrien's insistence. He wanted to get several shots of her done up for an Instagram page, which made her wonder at what point she would cross over into Bethany territory. She didn't mind being branded with a cleaned-up version of herself, but she did mind if she had to pretend to be someone she wasn't.

When Danny had walked across that dance floor with his eyes on her, she'd never felt so . . . so exposed. Men didn't chase her, men didn't ogle her, and men didn't cross a dance floor to pull her out.

When he'd first put out his hand to dance, she'd been irked and determined to call him out on his attitude. She put on a dress, and suddenly he couldn't take his eyes off her? Did he know how long it took for that transformation? Did he know how odd it felt for her? Sure, it was fun for a few hours, maybe once a month, but if that was what he expected in a woman . . .

But then he hadn't said a word about her appearance. Instead, he complimented her on the one thing that she was the proudest of. And the compliment had been genuine, or at least seemed like it.

Then she found herself spitting out some made-up excuse about taking photos of the lake to have a moment alone. She could hardly find her breath—what was she thinking?

They approached the paved path around the lake, neither of them speaking. Danny guided her to the right as the trail diverged in different directions. Her mind blanked, and she struggled to come up with something, anything to fill the silence. The investigation would make the most sense to talk about, but she wanted to forget about that for one night. "What made you become an FBI agent? I can't imagine that's an easy path. Did you always want to be one?"

"No, not exactly. I just wanted to be just like my pop."

The silence that filled the space between them wasn't awkward, and she didn't feel the need to talk as he found his next words.

"My father joined the Army when he was eighteen to fast-track his citizenship." Even in the moonlight, she could spot his pride. "My mother died when I was ten and he had to transfer out of active duty, but he was always on duty."

"I'm so sorry," she said, wishing she had better words. She couldn't imagine losing a mother at thirty, let alone ten.

He sighed. "It was a long time ago. The neighborhood I grew up in could be rough, and once she died, I started hanging out with the kids who didn't have any supervision. That's when my dad retired and our apartment became the Army."

"Did you have a bugle call at six a.m. every morning?"

He laughed, and the sound echoed across the water. "Five a.m., thank you very much. Man, I hated him for a while." The laughter faded. "When I was sixteen or so and watched my old friends disappear into the darkness, I started to appreciate him more. Then he died from cancer a year older than I am now."

She longed to call back his laughter, to bring him to a happier time. It made her drama over a stupid ring sound so minimal. "Why so young?"

"They don't know for sure, but the doctors said it could've been a result of fumes breathed in while serving overseas. After that, though, I knew I had to follow the man's example, or I'd wind up in jail or worse. I chose a path that was the exact opposite of where I felt like I was headed."

She reached out a tentative hand and took his arm, wishing it could be more. Her fingers slipped in between his elbow and body, and the warmth spread up her own arm.

"Long story short, I signed up for the ROTC to pay for a degree in criminal justice. I served my time in the Army as military police and then went straight to Quantico for training. I was going to chase terrorists."

"Was?"

"A few months after I graduated, a good friend from the neighborhood was convicted of drug dealing and got twenty years. The judge didn't care the 'dealing' had been fifty dollars exchanged between friends."

All these years later, she could feel his anger tense every muscle.

"Not long after, one of the attorneys who prosecuted my friend was charged with using his office to influence the outcome of several cases. He threw the cases of wealthy people who'd stolen a combined billion dollars and destroyed lives. Not one of them got more than a few years in jail, and some only fines. The rich people of the world don't follow the same laws as the rest of us."

Mirabelle thought of Bethany and her threats. If she didn't find the ring, the winner would be the one with the most money for lawyers. "You're right; they don't."

"I changed my focus to financial crimes, and I was really, really good at it."

With other men, his tone would've come out as arrogant, but Danny said it without any sense of bragging—only fact. For the first time all week, hope floated over the despair. Maybe having this man at her back wasn't such a bad idea after all. Guilt flowed through her at the distrustful way she'd treated him.

"What went so wrong at the FBI?" She almost hated to ask, but she had this strange sense she didn't want there to be any secrets between them.

"I wanted a bad man punished so much I didn't listen to warnings to back off. I focused all my attention on him. If I'd had better proof . . . but I couldn't get it and I couldn't let it go." He stopped walking and turned to face her. "You are really good at what you do, Mirabelle. But don't get so wrapped up in doing it you let go of everything else that matters. Even if we don't find the ring, your life still has to go on."

She started to tremble slightly, thinking of the black hole that would be like. "Has your life gone on? You don't seem that happy."

He took a breath. "No, but I'm working on it. Maybe I've been too focused on finding a new career and not building a new life. Chris offered me a position as a deputy, but I turned him down. I figured maybe it was time for something else."

"But you miss it."

"Only when I wake up, go to work, and go to sleep."

She laughed. "Sounds like you've completely moved on."

"Can I ask you a question?" He moved closer to her, and only the moonlight kept them apart.

Her breath caught. "Okay."

"Do you trust me?"

No secrets, she thought. "I didn't, but that has more to do with my own past than you." For the first time, she wondered how it would be to let go of that hurt.

"Who hurt you?"

"It's stupid, really." How could she go on about a bad break-up after hearing his life story?

"Mirabelle, I'd call you many things—loyal and stubborn among them—but not stupid."

"But I was." With a breath, she plunged in. "My ex, Eric, offered me up a big old diamond, and I thought everything was coming together. Then the day after we got engaged, he showed me our ten-year plan without any input from me. It had his career mapped out, what cities we would live in. He'd actually accepted an offer out in San Francisco without it occurring to him I might have an opinion about that."

"Did he not know you at all?" Danny scoffed.

She snorted in appreciation of his apt comment. "Apparently not. I stood there, stunned, and made a few comments about my own career, and he literally waved me off."

"Did you smack him down then or later?"

How did this guy know her better after a week than her so-called fiancé had after six months? "Later. I was so stunned, I sat there all quiet until he got up and left completely abuzz about our future. The sad thing was, I didn't even like the ring. I'm not even a fan of jewelry, but I slipped on the diamond and didn't say a word." She could still feel how heavy that ring had weighed.

"You have a complicated relationship with engagement rings."

Her laughter relieved the tension of the memories. They stopped their stroll on a wooden bridge crossing Emerald Creek, which fed the lake from the mountains. "I think I wanted it too much," Mirabelle said. "I wasn't happy at work, Tamyra had just gotten married, and I was so rudderless."

She shook her head to dispel a former self she hoped no longer existed. "I gave back the ring, quit my job, and moved away from the city. Within a few months, I found my land and never looked back. And I learned to be a lot more careful." She immediately regretted how bitter that last sentence sounded.

"Don't you trust yourself to not make the same mistake twice?"

"No, I don't." That was why she had to be so careful. She couldn't afford to be wrong a second time.

Across the water, a peal of giggles broke out.

Danny grabbed his flashlight. "Sorry. Looks like I've got to get back to work."

He took off down the bridge, leaving her a little lost in her thoughts and very confused about what had just happened.

"Hey." He paused on the path only a few yards away. "Do you want to go hiking tomorrow? I've been wanting to see the rest of that ridge."

She knew it wasn't a date—or was it? No. But a man couldn't have asked her out in a more fitting way. "Yes."

His face broke out into that charming yet aggravatingly mischievous way that she was finally starting to interpret. "Then it's a date."

14

A groggy Danny walked among the booths as the owners quickly set up for Saturday's big day. He blamed his blurry eyes on the late night patrolling the dance, but the quality of his sleep had suffered more than the quantity.

Every time he closed his eyes, he heard Mirabelle's voice. He'd told her stuff he hadn't told anyone—not in years. Being that vulnerable left him with competing senses of regret and relief. He needed to see her again to know which one would win out.

It was policy that whichever guards worked the dance did not have to work the day after. That made the previous night's shift a covetous one that his employees fought over. As the boss, he'd taken each one but then still worked the next morning. Today would be his first Saturday off since the festival had begun. He just needed to make one patrol of the area and make sure his people were in place before he could relax enough to go up the trail with Mirabelle.

Mirabelle. The thought of her quickened his step, and he was more than a little excited to spend the morning with her.

The sun crested the mountains, bringing a soft light but not yet warmth to the mountain valley. The morning mist over the grass cleared, and he spotted a giant booth filled with jars of honey and other products. A man wearing a sweater vest with shoulder-length blow-dried hair stood out front, directing where products ought to be placed. The vest did not fit in at all with the festival vendors, and Danny wondered if he'd finally spotted the elusive Tony, fiancé of Allie, and the only person there that night other than Bethany he hadn't spoken with.

Danny's requests to meet with him over the last few days had not been answered. He had a friend looking him up, but that friend hadn't had time to call him back. He wished he wasn't in a uniform. It would be easier to approach him as a customer, not as the law or sort of the law.

He plastered on a grin and walked up as if they were old friends. "Tony?"

The man's smile stayed, but his eyes went leery. "Yes?"

"I'm Mirabelle's friend. I've been helping her with the ring."

"Oh, of course." He glanced around, but for what reason Danny couldn't say. Guilt, looking for Allie, wanting to focus on customers? "Sorry we haven't been able to meet up."

Danny wanted to give him some reason to convince this guy to talk. "Oh, don't you worry about that. I'm new in town, but I've learned the festival takes priority over everything—especially a fake ring."

Tony's eyes widened, and he moved closer. "The ring's fake?"

"Do you have a second to talk?"

"Yeah, we have a couple of people to work the booth."

Danny followed Tony over to several tables in the food truck lot. They grabbed a few chairs and sat on the outer parameter.

Tony wasted no time, and he leaned closer. "So the ring's fake?"

"Okay, you didn't hear this from me." Danny glanced around "I don't know for sure, but who loses a half-million-dollar ring and doesn't file a police report? Plus, they won't answer any questions." The second part was true. Danny had left three messages with Bethany but hadn't had any responses.

Tony leaned back, nodding his head. "That makes sense. Who brings a ring that expensive on a horse ride?"

Danny kept an eye on Tony's reaction. He didn't spot any hint of disappointment. Maybe a degree of discomfort, but maybe also relief? "Yeah, at this point I think they're more embarrassed than panicked. We still need to find it, though."

"Yeah, perception is everything to people like that." Tony himself had more perception than Danny had expected.

Like with everyone, he had Tony walk him through the evening's events. He asked if he'd seen any other hikers or riders up on the ridge with them, but he said no.

"Maybe it's an insurance thing?" Tony offered.

His words sat Danny up straighter. "What do you mean?"

"They said it was a family ring, right?"

Danny nodded.

"Then they have an established record of owning it and probably have it insured. They can claim it went missing, and the insurance company has to pay up. But they can't afford to have the police look too close."

"They'd have to file a police report eventually."

"Maybe, but from what I heard, the family has influence. The company might not question well-paying clients too closely." He glanced around again. "I didn't tell Allie, but I was late that night because I was trying to track down some contacts I thought might know the fiancé's family. I figured they could put in a good word for me, and I could talk to him about investing in Sticky and Sweet."

Danny still couldn't figure out what a honey company needed with all these "investors." Was it in financial trouble? Had Tony found a better way to fund things? He really needed to get that report back from his friend.

In the meantime, the insurance theory wasn't exactly a bad idea. It would be nice to have the perp be someone everyone already disliked so immensely. He needed to dig into this with Bethany herself. He hadn't had any luck getting her on the phone. Maybe Adrien would be more helpful— if he could bring himself to call the Frenchman.

"Thanks," he said, still unsure whether this guy had given him a clue out of help or to get the attention off him. Either way, he'd pursue both leads. He did have one last question about who Bethany had talked to about being married for fifty years. "Did you by chance see her talking to Jameson?"

"Who's that?"

"The man cooking the food."

"The old guy?" He thought for a moment before nodding. "Yeah. In fact, they seemed to have a conversation right after Bethany came down. I remember wishing they'd get it over with so we could eat."

"And that was right before the ring went missing?"

"Sure, because we never did get the chance to eat. After that ring disappeared, all the *porcaria* hit the fan. Sorry, I'm Portuguese and sometimes I slip into my native tongue." He said that with a straight American accent.

Danny knew Spanish well enough to understand Portuguese and to know that this did not make sense. But it did give him more background for his friend to run this guy's past.

"Look, I've got to get back to the booth. They're going to open the gates in a few."

"Yeah, sure." Danny checked his watch; he had thirty minutes to make it out to the trailhead, where he'd have to ask Mirabelle again about Jameson.

Her uncle had sworn he hadn't talked to Bethany. Why would he lie? Maybe they could get to the bottom of what would probably be a simple explanation—he hoped.

irabelle didn't sleep, and then, when her alarm went off, she didn't eat. Had the conversation under the moonlight really happened? She tried to comb through her scattered thoughts to make sense of them but couldn't put them in any sort of order.

She hadn't expected Danny to open up about his own situation like that. She hadn't slept that night out of sheer confusion. She pushed her scrambled eggs around on her plate out of utter bafflement.

After she'd left the lake, she'd returned to Adrien, who'd promptly shown her six messages from Bethany demanding an update and effectively killing the mood. He'd taken that opportunity to push her to launch her own brand—with his help—using a whole lot of flattering words about her effervescent beauty.

Danny's words about his actual intentions had floated up, and she'd started to wonder if maybe he'd been right until she'd asked Adrien to dance in a desperate attempt to change the subject. He'd immediately taken two steps away from her and declared himself too tired and that it was time to head to the hotel. His rapid flight reminded her of all those boys back in college and high school: friendly enough as long she wasn't interested in them.

Mirabelle had spent the last night tossing and turning, rehashing every conversation she'd had with Danny. All her awkward flirtations at him must've made her look like a fool, but he was better at covering than Adrien. Of course he wasn't interested in her, which was just fine, because she wasn't interested in him.

Except when her phone beeped with a message from that very man, she nearly dropped it.

Ready to go?

Such a simple question with no good answer. She would go hiking with him, but for the first time in her life, she felt ill-equipped for such a venture. Would their conversation be more awkward after they had laid themselves bare the night before? Darkness had added a layer of protection to the conversation that would burn off in the light of day.

Then she remembered it was Saturday, and they only had two days to find the ring. It didn't matter what he thought of her, nor she of him, and she would keep the focus on that and only that.

A half hour later, she pulled into the public trailhead. Danny had said he wanted to walk the trail from the other side to get a feel for where other people could've come from. She didn't know whether to hope for or fear that outcome. If someone had snuck in and taken the ring, she had no hope of ever finding it.

He wasn't there yet, and she was grateful for a few minutes to pick the cotton out of her thoughts. No such luck. Before she could even turn off the ignition, his car slipped in beside hers.

She stepped out of the truck onto frozen mud. A low mist hovered over the mountains, giving her only a glimpse of what the day could bring. She zipped up her puffy purple jacket and yanked her beanie down tighter against the oncoming winter.

The exhaust from Danny's car lifted in a cloud before disappearing. He pushed open the door. "Good morning," he said with a chipper voice that did not belie *him* staying up all night thinking of her—a fact that irritated her far more than his bright voice.

She offered a casual yawn in response. "Sorry, late nights and I don't agree." They would keep it light.

"I'm with you. This festival has thrown off my sleep schedule."

She pulled a couple of Clif Bars out of her pack and offered him one. The cold air had brought back her appetite. Their breath filled the cold air.

"How long until it snows?" he asked as he unwrapped his bar.

If he only wanted to talk about the weather, then fine with her. "We usually get a few storms in November that melt off. The real storms don't start until December, but this year . . ." She shook her head. "This year feels different."

"What do you do in the winter to make money?"

"Whatever I can." That "whatever" included waitressing, cashiering, and any temp work she could pick up. "During Christmas, I do some sleigh rides. I'd like to eventually build something on the property large enough where I could host dinner parties and such, but that's down the road."

He slipped on a backpack and tightened the straps. The fact that he didn't wear a hydration pack like her and every other hiker and instead carried a little water bottle in these mountains marked him as a newbie. *He's going to need to buy one,* she thought, but then she remembered his temporary status.

"What are you going to do once the festival is over? I know you said you didn't want to be a deputy," Mirabelle asked, trying to muffle the stupid disappointment in her voice.

His face hardened. "I don't know." A hint of frustration crept into his voice. "It's not that I don't want to be a deputy. It's just . . . it's fine."

She realized she walked on shaky ground and wanted to call back her question. She'd been right; he would act like last night never happened. He probably regretted it, not wanting to give her the wrong idea about the two of them. Well, she didn't have the wrong idea and would play it cool. "I'm sure you'll figure it out."

He forced a lighter tone. "It's alright. I should've moved on from the FBI a long time ago. The hours were terrible and the pay barely sustainable in the city. I'll do much better in the corporate world." He spoke as a man trying to convince himself of something.

"I worked the corporate world, and I made good money." She forced a bright tone as she picked up her hydration pack from where she'd set it against a rock and strapped it on, and they started up the trail. The sun peeked out through the mist, promising warmer temperatures. "A lot of people like it."

"But not you?" His tone held genuine interest.

"Tamyra loved it. I think she still misses it. I knew my time was up when

I started dreading Saturday nights because the next day would be Sunday and then back to work."

"What finally pushed you out?"

"The whole 'breaking up with the fiancé' thing."

"Oh, sorry." He glanced down, looking embarrassed about something, but what it was she couldn't say. He probably didn't like the reference to the previous night.

"It's okay. I had no one to blame but myself. I had never, not once, told him what I wanted or what I thought. The few times I tried, I could tell us not agreeing bothered him, and I changed the subject." She tried to hold on to a casual tone. "It's over and done."

The trail started the slow rise to the ridge next to a meadow, which was usually green but now a soft shade of yellow.

"You really think you hold all the blame? Did he ever ask you what you wanted?"

The shoulders she had wrapped around her ears relaxed so slightly. Why did he have to sound so sympathetic? She couldn't figure him out.

Mirabelle flashed back to Eric and the hundreds of times they'd eaten together, gone out together, done anything together—realization dawning. "I guess he would, but if it wasn't something he wanted, he'd do his darnedest to talk me out of it." She'd been so afraid of making the same mistake twice, she hadn't realized the signs were there all along.

"What did you want?" Danny asked.

"This," she said, gesturing to the mountains around her. "I just wanted to be out here as much as possible." The horses, the barn, those were just the tools she used, but it came down to being in the mountains.

"Here's pretty good." The mud under their feet grew soft. Danny slipped a little, grabbing her sleeve for balance but immediately releasing it. "Sorry."

Very much aware of his nearness, she pressed on. "So, Agent Danny, forget the old job and forget the future jobs. What did you like to do?"

They reached a narrow steep part of the trail, and he slipped into step behind her, making talking awkward as he huffed his way up. She paused when it flattened while he caught his breath. "I like helping people," he said after a moment, "especially the ones who couldn't save themselves."

"Will you be able to do that in the jobs you're looking into?"

"No," he admitted. "But I can do other stuff I couldn't do before—like have a family."

A family? That came out of nowhere and poked a sore spot for her. A family was another thing she'd sacrificed in her goals, but she hadn't allowed herself to consider if that meant forever or just for now. "FBI agents don't have families?"

"They do. I guess I just knew I couldn't do both well. Not with the travel and the hours."

Despite her best efforts, Mirabelle found herself stepping closer to him. The formality slipped away, and the intimacy returned, along with a strong dose of terror. What was she doing?

"I've been avoiding another relationship because I thought being in one meant giving up on me. Maybe everything doesn't have to be all or none?"

He took a step closer to her and leaned in slowly. Was he going to kiss her? Her breath caught. Was she going to let him? She wanted to, wanted a release for the slow heat building inside of her. Wanted to feel wanted, even if it was for only a short time.

"Look," he whispered, his eyes on the meadow behind her.

She turned, her lips slightly apart. A pony with a thick red coat and black mane emerged from the mists—a foal trotting beside it. Two more heads emerged, the thump of the hooves echoing in the morning air. It took a moment to shake off the kiss that hadn't happened. What would she have done had he gone for it? Not an answer she had at her fingertips. "They're the wild ponies. They live up here."

"Where did they come from?" His voice held the wonderment of all who'd spotted the ponies for the first time.

"Nobody knows for sure. The story goes that ranchers back in the forties bred ponies that could survive alone in the mountains and used them to control the forest growth. Every fall they round up the herds, give them shots, and cull a few out to keep the numbers down."

"How did I not know about this?"

"They don't often come over here. This group must've traveled farther out."

They sat on a boulder, staring for a time at the wonder. Mirabelle took some photos, knowing it would make for a good Instagram post and hating that this thought was in her mind.

"That one we call Fabiette," she said, pointing at a palomino with a blond mane. "There was a stallion who looked a lot like him, and they nick-named him Fabio because of his luscious locks flowing behind him and his multiple foals each season. He was quite the ladies' man—er, horse."

"You're kidding me."

"Nope. He hasn't been seen in years, so everyone figured he died. Now any pony that has that same coloring and long mane gets called after him." She leaned slightly against his shoulder as they watched, content just to be close. How long had it been since she'd shared her personal space with a man—a man she trusted, even? Too long. He seemed to need the same thing as his hand brushed hers.

Before anything else could happen, Danny stood and broke the mood of the moment. "Okay, so if I'm a would-be thief out on the trail, how do I find out about the ring? How do I then steal it?"

She stood up, her mouth open without the words to fill it. Had this entire morning been about the ring? *Of course it was, you fool. You have two days.* She shook her head to dispel the emotions that kept pulling her in every direction. The focus should be on her company. If she lost that, nothing else mattered. "I don't know. We're getting close to the ridge."

She took the lead without turning around, her fists clenched by her side. The pines grew thick around them, concealing the view. She stopped at a fork in the trail and pointed down another tree-arched path. "That's where we come up."

He stopped and turned around. "Wait, so the trails don't join until here? How far are we from the top?"

"Fifteen minutes on foot, faster with the horses." Her voice was all business now.

"With the trees as thick as they are and the rocky ground, there's no going off the trail through here?"

"Nope. Once we reach the ridge, then everyone can spread out, but not before." She kept going, but he lingered a bit before following.

Danny broke through the silence a few minutes later. "Oh, I finally talked to Tony yesterday."

She stopped and turned back. "Anything helpful?"

"No, but he did mention something that surprised me. He said Bethany talked to Jameson."

"He said he didn't."

"Is there a reason Jameson wouldn't tell you about it?"

"Tony's not exactly . . ."

"What?"

She took a deep breath. "I don't think he's the most accurate source."

"He's marrying your friend. Don't you trust him?"

Before their engagement, Tony had charmed everyone but her, which didn't mean much with her attitude and trust issues. After the engagement, though, she started to spot dismissive behavior that was too similar to her own failed relationship. "Not necessarily. He's one of those people who like to make a story bigger than what it was."

"Maybe, but going by Bethany's Instagram story about talking to a long-married person, I think she spoke to Jameson, which he didn't tell us about."

The accusation froze in the cold air between them. Disappointment flared up, and she bristled. "You're calling him a liar? If you knew him, you would know how absolutely preposterous that is."

"Not a liar, just mistaken." He closed the distance between them, close enough he could touch her, but he didn't—lucky for him. "I have to be honest. After seeing the trail up, I don't think an outsider would've been able to get to the ring without someone noticing them. I don't see how they'd even know to steal it."

"They could've snuck—"

"But why? They would've had to know the ring existed and that there would be a chance to steal it. The only way a stranger taking it makes sense is if they happened upon it. If that were the case, someone would've noticed them."

A wall of denial rose up in her. "We have to find it. You said you would help me."

"I am. I think we should go talk to Jameson."

"And say what?" Her voice rose in panic and defensiveness, echoing off the mountains. "That he's a liar and a thief?"

"I didn't say that."

"You said he *lied*. And the only reason I can think of for him lying would be if he stole it." Anger replaced the disappointment. All Danny's talking today was a buildup to him accusing Jameson of the ring. He'd done to her what he did to everyone else—be all engaging while gathering information. And she'd been the stupid fool who'd fallen for it.

He stuttered over his words. "I said mistaken. I just think we should talk to him."

"No, you think you should interrogate him."

The stutter left his voice. "I told you from the start that I would follow this where it leads."

Mirabelle took two steps back. Her eyes flashed a warning sign. "And I told you that no one on that trip I know stole that ring. I'd sooner believe I took it than Jameson."

"I'm not going to ask him if he stole it; I'm only going to ask him if he talked to Bethany."

"No, you're not." If Bethany was going to bring down Mirabelle, then so be it. But she would fight with her last breath before Danny would bring down her family. "I don't need your help anymore."

Mirabelle took off down the trail at a rate that Danny couldn't keep up with. With his lowlander lungs, he had no chance against someone who ran these trails each day for morning exercise. Perhaps ditching him was the childish move, but she couldn't bear descending for an hour or more making small talk with someone who could betray her like this. Plus, she wanted to get to Jameson before he could and give him a heads-up.

Danny wouldn't stop. He couldn't let a crime go to save his FBI job, let alone walk away because she asked him to. Even if it meant ruining anything that had grown between them.

Her truck sprayed mud behind the large tires as she roared away from the trailhead.

16

Danny made it down the mountain, angry at Mirabelle for ditching him and more frustrated at himself for getting distracted by her. Despite his best intentions, he'd leaned in to kiss her. At the last moment, he found his senses and grabbed on to the nearest other distraction—the ponies.

He should walk away—that was what she wanted, after all—and that was what he was determined to do. Except he found himself loading up on gas and Gatorade and hitting the road to Virginia Beach, where the elusive Bethany had tagged her location in an Instagram story—her first since he'd been checking her feed.

He called Adrien from the road just to confirm. "Is she there, or are these old pictures?" he asked.

Adrien lowered his voice. "I shouldn't tell you."

"Come on. You don't want Mirabelle to go down for this, do you? Or you?"

"No, but . . ."

"I won't tell her how I found out. I'll attribute it to my own amazing detective skills."

Adrien laughed. "Fine. I'll text you the directions."

Danny drove out of the mountains, wondering why in the world he was helping a woman who so clearly did not want him to. There was only one reason: he didn't like leaving a case unsolved, and that was it. It had nothing to do with Mirabelle or her smile or how easy it was to talk to her. It was just . . .

He slammed his hand into the steering wheel at her absolute stubbornness and loyalty. That woman Bethany would destroy her, and he couldn't let that happen. Not when he could protect her.

A few hours later, Danny stood outside a small restaurant overlooking the ocean, staring at his phone waiting for a response from Adrien. The fall temps made for a quieter-than-usual Saturday. Between the gray clouds and the churned ocean, it was impossible to tell where the water ended and the sky began.

He texted Adrien but received no response. After twenty minutes, he walked down the sidewalk lining the beach scanning the sand for some sign of the woman he'd only seen in pictures.

She turned out to be much easier to spot than he'd imagined. While she was the only woman on the cool day on the beach wearing a bikini, it was the entourage that grabbed his attention: two people with cameras, one person with a white light screen, and a woman with clothes on a hanger followed her across the sand. As Danny got closer, he recognized Adrien as one of the photographers. At least the man hadn't led him astray.

He stopped about fifty feet off to observe the parade. How much money was the woman getting from posting nonsense to afford this? They stopped the shooting, and Adrien turned and spotted him. He said something to Bethany that was lost in the roar of the ocean.

She looked at Danny up and down, clearly finding him wanting. She, however, wanted for nothing. Her blonde ringlets cascaded over a perfectly toned body. She was a walking advertisement for everything a person could want—until he got too close and she came into focus. Bethany held that same look of cold calculating he'd spotted in so many people he'd sat across an interview table from.

After measuring Danny for a moment, she plastered on a smile, trying to warm him up. The woman with the extra clothes wrapped Bethany in a robe, but Bethany waved her off from tying it tight. She strode towards him with a confidence he couldn't help but admire. This was a woman who knew what she wanted and would probably get it.

He inventoried his options with how to approach this conversation and chose the only one that would work with her. With a brief glance, he made eye contact and then immediately turned his eyes to the sand, faking embarrassment.

"Danny," she said with a quiet voice and a soft Southern accent. According to his prior research, she'd been born in Iowa and had only moved to the South to attend college in Charleston at age twenty. Her social media pages billed her as @ByWayOfBethany, a guru of everything young, hip, and Southern.

"Bethany." He lifted his eyes and offered an admiring smile. "It's so nice to finally meet you. I'm here to help."

"Thank you so much for what you're doing to find my ring. Adrien here said you're quite the private investigator and a former FBI agent to boot. I'm awfully glad to have you." She would play the damsel in distress to the big strong man, acting very welcoming for a woman who hadn't returned any of his calls.

"Is there a place we can talk?" He glanced around at the others. "In private." He emphasized the last word.

"How about I let you buy me lunch?" she said with a wink.

"It would be my pleasure." He really hoped she was one of those women who refused to eat more than a lettuce leaf in front of a man. He had a feeling he couldn't afford Bethany on a security guard's salary.

Luckily, with the way she was dressed, she chose a beachside sandwich shop. She kept her robe only loosely drawn.

"Tell me," she said, reaching for his hand and giving it a squeeze, "what have you found out so far?"

He considered what he could tell this woman and what he couldn't. There wasn't much he dared say; she'd be the type to go off unhinged at anyone remotely connected. "We're considering the possibility that someone, perhaps a fan, may have followed you up. I've talked to a few people who saw your live story."

He'd come here today because he wanted to finally meet her, to see if there was any truth to what Tony had proposed about the insurance. And he fed her this story because he wanted to see what her response to it would be.

"I don't know," she said slowly. "I posted my story right before we set out. I don't know how someone could catch up with us."

Interesting that she didn't jump right on that explanation. If she were guilty, she'd want to point the finger at everyone.

"Plus, there weren't many people on the trail," she continued. "I specifically chose a Monday to ensure we wouldn't have crowds interfering with the shoot."

Mirabelle had been right when she'd said Bethany had planned out her entire engagement. He couldn't help but notice she called her engagement a "shoot."

"I know Ms. Mason believes a squirrel carried it away, perhaps attracted by how shiny it was." He purposely distanced himself from Mirabelle to get Bethany to trust him more and to take the heat off her. Bethany was already on Mirabelle's case; she didn't need any more ammunition, and Danny would do all he could to take the target off her back.

She scoffed. "Really, a squirrel." She leaned across the table, allowing her robe to come open. "Do you believe that, Danny? Is it alright if I call you that?"

He wished he had Mirabelle's ability to blush—that would've sold his smitten routine better. "Of course. And I want to do everything possible to find your ring. I know that you wanted to keep this private, but if I find the . . ."

"Honey, all I want is the ring back. If whoever has it hands it over, there'll be no questions asked."

Interesting, a half-million-dollar ring and no charges. Somehow, he doubted that. "Could you tell me more about it? I'd like to make some discreet inquiries to dealers who might spot it. If someone did steal it, they will have to sell it eventually."

"And you promise you will be discreet? I don't want to file a report unless, of course, you know for sure someone stole it."

"I swear."

"It's just . . ." She glanced down, feigning innocence and worry. "Can I confide in you, Danny?"

"I'd like to think you can trust me with anything." It was his turn to lean close and bat his eyes.

"My fiancé's family doesn't think much of me."

"Why on earth not?" It was getting hard to keep his tone in the realm of sincerity and not sarcasm.

"Because I didn't come from money. I've had to work very hard to get to where I am. They come from old Massachusetts money and consider me a gold digger." She blinked back a few tears. Real or not, he couldn't say for sure.

He patted her hand in comfort. "And the ring is theirs?"

"It's mine; I earned it." That statement seemed to startle her as much it did him. He figured that was her true self popping up at an inopportune moment. "I just mean I love my fiancé so much. If they find out about the ring, they'll never approve of the marriage. In fact, they may even accuse *me* of stealing it." She sniffed and managed to pump her chest as she made gasping noises.

Danny understood now why Mirabelle would carry the blame if he couldn't find it—Bethany couldn't watch everything she'd worked for go down the drain. "What does your fiancé say?"

"Oh, bless his heart. He's been such a gem through all this. He's even suggested we get a replacement made until we find it." Her face hardened, clearly not willing to relinquish the heirloom. That ring represented everything she'd worked for. The woman was like a demented Girl Scout after the badge at all costs.

After their lunch, they took to the boardwalk, where her crew was setting up for the next shoot. As they walked, she slipped an arm through Danny's, and he had to stop himself from pulling away. He never had liked snakes. "Do you think you'll find it?" she asked.

"I'll do my very best, but I'm not sure if it'll turn up in the next few days." He wanted to buy some time.

Her arm tightened. "I would hate to think anyone from that night stole it. They were such nice people."

"In my experience, even nice people make mistakes."

"Of course." She paused for a moment. "*If* the ring doesn't come back in time, or if my future family were to somehow find out about it, I can't protect who took it. You understand?"

He did, clearly. Bethany would easily and gladly put the blame on whomever she could to deflect it away from herself. They had less than two days to find the ring, and they had to hope her fiancé kept his parents from finding out it was lost. "One last question: do you remember talking to Jameson that night?"

"I'm not sure." She delicately tapped her chin with a bright red nail.

"He's an older gentleman with gray hair—the cook."

"Oh, yes. I remember thinking he looked like the epitome of a Southern gentlemen. We talked for a second before dinner. I was going to ask him for marriage advice but then Adrien interrupted. Why?"

"I've been trying to place everyone."

"Well, it couldn't be him. He was down below while we were still shooting."

Unexpected relief washed through Danny. He would call Mirabelle and tell her the good news, except now . . . he didn't have a whole lot of suspects. He would have to start over.

He walked Bethany back to the others, where she joined the stylist, who started fussing over her hair. Adrien broke free and joined him on the boardwalk. "Any luck?"

"Bethany would cut off her own finger off before she'd let that ring go."

Adrien nodded. "Yes, I am afraid of what she'll do. My wife wants me to get on the next plane to avoid the consequences."

"Why don't you?" Danny's head swung around as he digested the words. "Wait, your wife? I didn't know you were married."

"Oh, yes, we have five years and four children." Adrien broke into a smile at that crazy math.

"I checked out your Instagram, and I didn't see any family."

"My wife, ironically, is very private. She will not let me photograph the children." He pulled out his phone and brought up the backdrop, which displayed his grinning family and a shy woman focused more on the children than the camera.

"Is it hard to do your work and raise a family?" Danny asked, his eyes on the babies and toddlers. Mirabelle had been right when she'd said the man wasn't flirting with her. He was just so . . . so French.

"Yes, very." Adrien shrugged and put the phone away. "I work very hard to minimize the impact on them."

"Why not change careers?"

"To what, my friend? I am very good at what I do." He said this matter-of-factly but without bragging. "It is not ideal, but nor is any job. We live but one life; why not try to do it all?"

"Adrien." Bethany's strident tone carried across the sand. "We're ready."

"Some days," Adrien whispered, "it is much less than ideal."

"Hey, when you have a second, can you send me the photos from earlier in the night before the proposal?" Bethany's Instagram story about meeting someone who had been married fifty years still gnawed at him.

"Adrien, are you coming?" Bethany yelled again.

"Tomorrow, my friend, first thing."

Danny hit the highway back to the mountains and Mirabelle. He would find the ring and return it to Bethany; getting justice was what he did very well.

Mirabelle called Jameson a few times but got no response before remembering he'd taken Isabelle out of town for the day. She could wait until they got back, relieved Danny couldn't ruin their weekend.

That left her with a few hours to kill before she had to get home and prep for Saturday evening's ride. After leaving the trail, she pointed her truck and headed into town. She didn't want to go to the festival and risk running into Danny. She had nothing to say to him, but she did have a whole lot she wanted to say to Tamyra. With the festival coming to a close soon, Tamyra would be there all day.

The pie booth was hopping when Mirabelle got there, and she gladly stood in line for a chance for some warm apple pie à la mode.

"Hey, Mirabelle, how are you?"

She turned to spot a woman she vaguely recognized. She transformed to host mode immediately and slapped on a smile. "Hi there, how are you?"

"A little disappointed we weren't able to book a night with you this festival."

The memories slid in along with a name: Jessica, a former guest. "I'm so sorry. Why not?" It wasn't like she was booked solid.

"Oh, it's not your fault. We couldn't decide on whether we were coming until the last minute, but next year for sure."

A man walked up, and Jessica turned to greet him, leaving Mirabelle to stew in her thoughts. This was the second year she'd offered the romantic horseback rides. The first year, she'd done them on Friday nights only. This year she'd expanded it to three days a week. How big could she grow with one more year?

If Bethany trashed her, would her customers come back? Would they be loud enough to shout out the angry reviews?

"Mirabelle."

She shook off her thoughts to face Tamyra, who held out a piece of apple pie. Who could ask more from a best friend than that?

"Mama!" Tamyra shouted over her shoulder. "I'm taking a break." She undid her apron and came around the booth, where she joined Mirabelle.

"Thanks," Mirabelle said as she took the slice of heaven. "Do you have a second to talk?"

"After I pee."

Mirabelle took the opportunity to cast a glance at the tiny little being protruding from Tamyra's usually flat stomach. What a lucky baby to come to such a family.

The line for the bathroom stretched around the brick building and down the row of booths. Tamyra rubbed her baby and loudly exclaimed how hard it was to be pregnant. Magically, the line parted, and they made their way to the next open stall. "Works every time," she whispered before slipping inside.

Mirabelle downed her piece of pie while she waited outside. Tamyra popped back out, and they walked down the main drag to the edge of the park where the crowds thinned.

"Well?" Tamyra said, her eyes dancing with the anticipation of a good story.

Mirabelle's mood soured quickly. The story wasn't all that great, and the prince was less than charming. "Well what?"

"I take it you took my advice, going by what all happened last night."

"Last night?" The memory of the dance felt like days ago, not the night before.

"Did you not see the way he looked at you? You think he liked the dress?"

"No," she said quite honestly. "But I think he liked the dance."

"Are y'all going to go out?"

Maybe realizing she had no chance at anything with him made her honest with herself for the first time. "No, it's not going to work." She took a deep breath. Why did she care?

"It's okay," Tamyra said, wrapping an arm around her for a side hug. "You knew it was going to end anyhow. I hope you had some fun."

"I liked him," Mirabelle blurted out. "He noticed me in a way other men haven't. And it's so stupid. It's only because he's a cop, and he's super observant. I'm like those women who fall for their therapists because they finally have a man who listens to them. Am I that pathetic?"

"Oh, honey. This is completely different. You liked him and, going by what I saw, he liked you. Maybe the timing isn't right, but that happens."

"You really think he did?" It was one thing for him to see her for who she was; it was another thing if he liked her anyhow. A lot of men weren't attracted to a woman who knew what she wanted and wasn't going to bend her life to meet theirs. Not to mention there weren't a lot of single men left.

"Are you sure you won't see him again?"

"I don't want a relationship."

"No, you're scared of a relationship."

"I'm scared of losing myself."

"That doesn't have to happen."

Then Mirabelle said the one thing she'd been trying not to since Tamyra had quit her job. "Everyone does. Every woman I know has given up a part of herself for a guy. Even you." The second she said it, she wished she could undo it. But you couldn't call back a flood.

"What's that supposed to mean?" Tamyra stood to her full height, her hands on her hips.

"You quit the job you loved when you got married."

"So? That was a choice I made for my own happiness; Ty didn't make me. If you're implying I'm weaker because of it, then we're going to have words."

"Come on," Mirabelle blurted out, because the damage was already done. "You loved your career, you were finally moving up, and now you audit the books of a small town. You can't tell me that was your dream. I don't want to wake up one day and realize I've lost myself again."

"First of all, Mirabelle, dreams change. What I wanted ten years ago isn't what I want now. And ten years from now, who knows? Maybe I'll be back on the fast track. The point isn't to choose someone who supports you right now; it's to choose someone who supports you through it all. Just because you chose the wrong guy doesn't mean I did."

Tears burned at the back of her eyes as shame flooded through her. It was so much easier to think the problem was with everyone and not just her. "I'm sorry, Tamyra. You're right; I'm just so scared that someone like that doesn't exist for me."

Besides providing pie, the other thing a best friend did well was forgive. Tamyra wrapped her arms around her and pulled her into a hug. "I wish I could promise he does, but I can't." She pulled back, and her eyes found Mirabelle. "But I can promise you will never find him if you don't trust yourself to have learned better. Now, why don't you allow yourself to have a little fun with this guy without worrying so much?"

"It's not going to happen." She caught Tamyra up on everything that had occurred that morning.

"I don't know why you're so upset," Tamyra said. "Jameson probably just forgot he'd talked to her. Why are you so worried?"

"I'm not," she added sharply.

Tamyra shot her a look calling her out.

"There's something I never told you about Jameson, something I never told anyone." Mirabelle took a breath. She walked down the sidewalk at a slow pace with Tamyra beside her.

Tamyra didn't reply but instead waited. Mirabelle didn't have to ask her best friend to keep her confidence. Had it been her secret to tell, she would've told her a long time ago.

"A few years ago," she started haltingly, "Jameson's business hit a wall and he lost a lot of money on some bad investments." A group of revelers passed them and waved. She waited for them to disappear into the crowds before continuing. "He lost everything."

"Wait, Jameson lost his business? I thought he sold it. Everyone said it was enough to last him a lifetime."

"He lied." Mirabelle cringed at that word. "It was a harmless lie to save face. Not even Aunt Isabelle knows the truth. She was diagnosed about the same time."

"And that's why he's been cooking for you?"

"Yeah, everyone figured he was doing it as a favor, but . . ."

"How did you find out?"

"He asked me to go over the numbers."

Tamyra stopped, but Mirabelle couldn't lift her eyes up to face her. "A lie to save face is a whole lot different from stealing—especially if that stealing would hurt you," Tamyra said.

Mirabelle squeezed her eyes shut against the knowledge she wished she could forget.

"What else?" Tamyra asked.

"It was the same guy who took Allie's dad down. He saw how much shame he went through and decided to keep it quiet. The investments weren't illegal exactly, but they were get-rich-fast type schemes."

"And you think Jameson saw the opportunity to get rich fast again?"

"No," Mirabelle said quickly. "No, I just . . ."

"You're just afraid, as unlikely as it is, you might be wrong."

"Danny said something when all this started that no one knows their loved ones as well as they think they do." She'd been mad at him for that, because hadn't she known almost everyone there that night for almost her entire life? "I didn't think Jameson was the type to give money to a scammer, but he did. What if . . . what if I don't know him like I thought I did?"

The clouds moved, and the sun broke through and shone on them. "You have to ask him," Tamyra said.

"I know. I just don't know what to do with his answer. If he says he didn't take it, will I believe him?" She took a deep breath and swallowed. "And if he did take it, what then?"

"Then you can return it and get your life back."

"And live my life knowing the one person I look up to more than anyone could hurt me so much. How do I get over that?" Her voice broke. "I'd rather lose my business than lose that."

Tamyra reached out and wrapped her in a tight hug and let her weep. After a few moments, she pulled back. "You have to ask Jameson."

"I know." She wiped her eyes and really wished she'd grabbed a wad of toilet paper from the bathroom. "You know what sucks?"

"What's that?"

"I really want to ask Danny his advice, but I don't dare. And I kind of, sort of told him where to go."

Tamyra squeezed her mouth shut, but laughs came out in shudders in her shoulders.

"Tamyra!"

"I'm sorry, but you're right, it sucks." Tamyra squeezed her arm. "But none of this may mean anything. Just ask Jameson."

"I know. I'll go over there tomorrow morning first thing. He left to take Aunt Isa to see some family over in Richmond, and I've got another dinner tonight." She didn't voice to Tamyra her other fear—tomorrow was Sunday, and the ring was due by Monday. If Jameson didn't have it, what other options were left?

* * * * *

Danny knew Mirabelle would hate him for thinking it, but he couldn't help but note similarities between her and Bethany. Both were self-made, attentive to detail, and their futures were each tied to a yellow stone.

He called Mirabelle twice on the road back home from the beach; the phone rang a few times before going straight to voicemail. One ring would've meant her phone was dead or she was on it. Several rings meant she didn't answer it for whatever reason. Two rings meant she was deliberately ignoring him.

He wanted to give her an update, but more than that, he just wanted to talk to her. He'd spoken with her at least a few times every day for the last five days and hadn't realized how attached he'd grown to her voice. The morning that had started off so promising had darkened fast.

Tony had been wrong. Bethany hadn't stolen the ring any more than Mirabelle had. She'd never wear some knockoff while the real one floated around. Danny did agree with her about the improbability of anyone coming up that ridge not part of the original group.

That left Tony and Allie, Tamyra and Ty.

On the third attempt to reach Mirabelle, he finally left a message. "I'm sorry about thinking Jameson lied. Please call me back; we're down to two days."

When he pulled into the sheriff's drive and his temporary home, he spotted Chris balancing his youngest son, a four-year-old, on his bicycle. He parked on the road so as not to block the driveway. "Looking good, Marc."

The boy had his tongue stuck out in complete concentration and couldn't reply to his honorary uncle. Danny watched them a bit, still in disbelief his friend had three kids out of diapers while he hadn't managed one.

After about a few minutes, Marc tipped over and climbed up to his feet. "I'm done," he announced in a very grown-up voice.

"Then you'd better go in and wash up for dinner." Chris swatted his behind in a loving gesture as he ran up the porch steps.

Danny came over. "My pop would've never let me stop after a fall." He didn't say this in judgment, only wonder.

"Mine either. We'd be out all night until I got it right." What had bonded them initially was equal parts resentment and love of their strict fathers. "But Marc won't have to fight his way through the world like we did."

"Good," Danny said with feeling.

"How did the job interview go?"

"Huh?" Then Danny remembered the only reason he'd leave town for hours at a time, up until last week. "I don't know."

"You don't know about the job or about changing careers?" Chris had offered him a job of deputy after he'd first gotten fired, but Danny had adamantly refused.

"I don't know."

Chris grabbed a rake and went after the falling leaves that seemed to have no end.

Danny grabbed a wheelbarrow to help. "Don't you miss the city?"

"No." He stopped and looked around the yard. "This town actually reminds me of the old neighborhood before it got all gentrified."

Danny scoffed. "This town?"

"You know how it was growing up. Everyone knew your name and your business, and we couldn't get away with nothing without it getting back to our parents."

"That's true. Remember Old Man Darius?"

Chris burst out laughing. "Don't remind me. My butt is still store from that swatting."

"Forget the swatting. Remember when he caught us stealing and said in that deep voice of his, 'My boys, if your families are struggling, all you have to do is ask.' I have never felt so much shame in my life." That included "quitting" the FBI.

"I forgot about his voice. Man, getting a lecture from him was like hearing the voice of God himself correcting you." He grabbed a pile of leaves and tossed them into the barrel. "You know he got bought out about ten years ago. Everyone did."

"I heard."

"How's it going with Mirabelle?" Chris asked.

He sighed. "I think I blew that one."

"What do you mean? Have you not found the ring?"

It took Danny a second to realize Chris referred to the investigation and not their nonexistent relationship. Of course, "relationship" was a bit of an exaggeration. "I hit a wall today. The one lead I had didn't pan out."

"It didn't pan out the way you wanted?"

He thought on that for a minute. "No, it didn't pan out the way I expected." He stopped with a handful of leaves, considering the conversation with Bethany. "Except what if I made the wrong assumption . . ." He dropped the leaves in the wheelbarrow and turned to his apartment over the garage.

"Danny."

"What?"

"You've been out of work two months and you've spent all your time working the festival or working this case. You sure your future is down the private path?"

"Why are you asking?"

Chris pulled a piece of paper out of his pocket and handed it to Danny. "I got a call today from someone trying to track you down about a job offer. He said you served together, and he had an offer only an idiot would refuse."

Danny stared at the slip of paper, contemplating how big of an idiot he was.

18

irabelle pulled up to Jameson's house right after seven Sunday morning but didn't spot his SUV in the driveway, only her cousin Jimmy's car. With one knock on the door, she opened it and called out, "Hello." No one in their family waited to be formally welcomed in.

"Mirabelle," Jimmy came out of the kitchen. "How are you? How are the dinners going?"

"Fine. I think I'm going to have to train someone to take over on a more permanent basis for next year. I know Uncle Jameson loves it, but . . ."

Jimmy nodded sadly. "Mom's taking more and more of his attention. He ran to get groceries for the church's monthly breakfast. She's in her craft room doing some sewing if you want to visit."

"I'll go on back."

Mirabelle couldn't have been more different than her namesake. Isabelle had grown up in the traditional South, where a woman had a certain place, and she never questioned that place. Mirabelle's own mother and Isabelle's sister, born fifteen years and another generation later, had taken a slightly different route. That less-traveled road—at least back then—had taken her to college, a job, and later a family.

There had always been some friction between the two sisters. Isabelle sometimes still tried to mother her younger sister into more "traditional" ways, but that always gave out to love. While she sometimes looked at Mirabelle and her "crazy" choices, she'd done so with pride along with the confusion.

Isabelle sat at the sewing machine, staring at a piece of white fabric in her lap. Mirabelle cleared her voice from the doorway. "Aunt Isabelle."

Despite her quiet tone, the lady jumped in her seat. "Oh my goodness, child, you startled me."

"Sorry." The bright yellow room carried the full afternoon sun, warming it from the outside chill. Mirabelle pulled out a chair from a desk and sat next to her aunt. "What are you sewing?"

Her eyes returned a blank answer until she glanced down at her lap. "Oh, yes. Just putting some monograms on a handkerchief." Traditional lady indeed.

All the questions she had about the ring and that day would wait until Jameson got home.

Isabelle passed her a few fabric swatches. "Do you want to iron these?" She gestured to a little ironing board on the cutting table.

Mirabelle plugged in the iron and waited for it to warm up.

"Who was that man the other night?" Isabelle asked with a faked casualness Mirabelle could spot from yesterday.

"What man?" Why did her aunt's memory have to be so darn good when it came to things she didn't want to talk about?

"Don't be petulant. You know exactly who you danced with."

Mirabelle kept her eye on the board. "Just someone I met recently."

"Oh, really? He's very handsome."

"He's not that good-looking," Mirabelle muttered.

"Oh, not in the way of classic handsomeness, but he carries himself in a way that says he knows who he is and what he wants. It's very drawing."

Mirabelle flipped over the first swatch and chewed on Isabelle's opinion for a second before deciding to take advantage of her aunt's fading memory and get some help in the romance department. "What did you think about Uncle Jameson when you first met him?"

Isabelle glanced around as if someone would overhear them. "Well, truth be told, I didn't think much of him at all."

"What?" Mirabelle couldn't help but laugh.

"He was trying so hard to impress me that it came off as arrogance. After the third story about his prowess on the football field, I asked him to take me home."

"What changed your mind?"

"He showed up the next day with a single daisy and apologized. Said he was so very nervous about impressing me and asked for one more chance. He proposed at the next festival. By then, I thought much more of him," she said with a sly smile.

"What made you fall in love with him?"

"I had lots of boys chasing me back then."

Mirabelle could believe it. She'd seen pictures of her aunt back then, and she'd had a beauty to be noticed.

"And I thought he was just like the others strutting around, but on our second date, he shut up and listened."

"Aunt Isabelle!" That was the equivalent of other people using the F-word.

"What can I say? It's refreshing to date a man who cares what you think, who has respect for your opinion." She shook her scissors at Mirabelle. "That should be the bare minimum of dating a fellow."

Mirabelle had to agree. "How did he propose?" She thought of the overly engineered proposal she'd witnessed that week. "Was it romantic?"

"Of course." A brilliant smile crossed her face. "Mostly because I wanted so much to say yes, but partly because he'd saved for months to buy me the most beautiful yellow ring—as bright as this room."

Mirabelle's head jerked up and she scooted her chair to her aunt's. "I didn't know the ring was yellow." Truth be told, she'd never paid any attention to her aunt's ring.

"Of course you knew that. I hardly ever remove it." She glanced down at her finger. "I must've taken it off for sewing." She shook her head as if to clear the memories.

Mirabelle suddenly remembered the old ring. It had been lost during the same time Jameson lost his company. With all the craziness of the time, she barely had a memory of her mother helping Isabelle search her house.

She debated how upset the next question would make her aunt if she was right about the ring being lost. Not worth it, and she decided to wait for Jameson. "I'm going to make us some iced tea. Does that sound good?"

"I suppose." Mirabelle hadn't made it to the door before the bright voice behind her called out. "Oh, here it is. I put it in my little treasure drawer."

She turned to see her aunt holding out a giant yellow ring that Mirabelle had last seen on the finger of the woman who would ruin her life. She squeezed her eyes shut as if that would block out the knowledge of how wrong she'd been.

"Do you feel all right, dear?"

Mirabelle opened her eyes to see her aunt's innocent and wholly unaware gaze on her as she put on the ring. She stumbled backward. "I don't . . . I have to . . ." She ran out the door, oblivious to anything but the searing pain brought on by one thought.

Danny had been right all along. If only she'd listened.

* * * * *

Before Danny could get dressed Sunday morning, his phone pinged with two messages. Since neither was from Mirabelle, he ignored them both until he got out of the shower.

Fully awake, he stared at both messages. One had a link to the images from before the proposal; the other was from his old buddy about a job.

He did the smart thing for a change and called his buddy back first.

"Beck Alstead," said the strident voice as way of hello. He and Beck had served overseas together.

"It's Danny Cabrera."

"I'm glad you called, and I won't waste your time with small talk. I'd heard you left the FBI and are job hunting. I have a private security firm and wanted to talk to you about a position."

Danny sat down at the card table that doubled as his kitchen table next to the hot plate that was his kitchen. "What kind of position?"

"It's actually a training job. I'm growing fast, and I'm taking on a lot of young people who just don't have the experience we do. Most of the seasoned vets are done with traveling, and I'm struggling to meet the needs of all my clients. The position would keep you in New York most of the time, and the starting pay would be 150K to start with."

He struggled to find his voice. "150K a year?"

"Yeah, I know it sounds a bit low, but you'll get a bonus per recruit we place with a client. That could tack on another 25K to your salary, and that's just the first year."

The deputy job Chris had offered him started at 50K.

Truth be told, the salary was a small jump over what he could've made even if he'd climbed the ladder at the FBI. But this was just a starting salary without the travel, the late nights, and the risk. He could settle down in one place, afford to buy an apartment in the neighborhood he'd grown up in, and start having a life.

"Let me send you over the link with the details," Beck said.

Danny pulled out his iPad and clicked the link that popped in his messaging app.

"Do you see it?"

"Yes," Danny said. Except he wasn't staring at a job listing; he was staring at the images from Adrien. He must've clicked on the wrong message.

"What do you think?"

He'd thought he'd accounted for everyone there that night, but he'd been wrong. "Can I give it some thought?"

"Of course. Why don't you come to New York next week and I can give you a tour and a more detailed offer?"

The job was already a distant thought as he stared closer at the photos. Much like the night he'd been there, the old Ford carrying the food and supplies sat parked a ways from the barn. In one group shot, a reluctant Jameson stood to the side, but in the background, Danny could spot the outline of a person's head in the Ford.

Jameson hadn't been alone.

He tried to call Mirabelle one more time but still reached her voicemail. "Mirabelle, I know Jameson didn't lie about talking to Bethany. Please, call me back. I think we can find the ring without pointing the finger at anyone."

He rushed to get dressed. If she wouldn't call him, he would find her.

19

Mirabelle sat on the porch awaiting Jameson's return. The ring now sat on Isabelle's finger, where it would not come off without a bit of coercion.

She'd debated pulling the ring off her aunt's hand, running to her truck, and driving all the way to Virginia Beach. She could place the ring in Bethany's tentacles and claim she'd found it somewhere. "Aren't we lucky?" she would say.

Bethany wouldn't want to pitch a fit or go to the police. She'd gladly take the ring, and they could disappear from each other's life. Mirabelle would never get her recommendation, and that would be fine. She'd built the business without it and had come this far, hadn't she?

Then why did she hesitate, waiting on the porch?

Outside her own parents, she trusted Jameson more than anyone. How could he lie to her? How could he watch her panic over that stupid ring and do nothing? Would he have watched her life fall apart and still remained silent? She would and could keep his name out of this, but before she did that, she had to know if he'd do the same for her.

The sun crested the mountains, bringing bright light to what should be a dismal day. Her aunt used to go all out in harvest decorations, filling the yard with bales of straw, scarecrows, and pumpkins. This had been the first year where none of the decor was put out. Mirabelle kept intending to come over and help, but the business kept pushing that intention further down the road.

Jameson pulled into the driveway and smiled through the windshield as he spotted her. How could he smile at her, knowing what he'd done? Before he even made it up the sidewalk with grocery bags in hand, tears filled her eyes.

He dropped the bags and rushed to her side. "What is it? What's wrong, sweet pea?"

At the name she hadn't heard in years, the anger overwhelmed the tears. "How could you lie to me? How could you destroy everything?"

His blue eyes widened in surprised. Had he thought she wouldn't figure it out? "What are you talking about?"

"Isabelle showed me the ring, Uncle Jameson. She told me you gave it to her. Did you see it sitting there and think it looked like the ring she lost?"

"What are you talking about?"

"The ring!" she shouted before lowering her voice. "The ring that is going to destroy everything I worked for. I understand you wanting to take it, but when that woman threatened me, how could you not say anything?"

"I don't know what you're talking about!" His voice rose to match hers.

"It's on her hand even as we're talking. You can't lie about this anymore."

He passed her, wrenching open the front door and leaving the screen slamming behind him. "Isabelle," he called out, his voice softened from the previous moment's anger. "Isa, darling. Where are you?"

Mirabelle left the light of the shadows of the porch and stood in the morning light, pushing back the tears that she didn't have time for.

Jameson returned to the porch a few minutes later, his shoulders hunched over. "She showed you the ring?"

"I just need it back. I'll tell Bethany I found it with a metal detector or something."

"That won't be the end of it," Jameson said, anger filling his voice. "That woman's vindictive. She'll still come after you."

"She may, but she can't prove I didn't find it. Only you and I know what really happened. That you stole it." He flinched at those words, but she couldn't help the dig. How could he?

"No." He emphasized that word. "I'll drive it down today."

"With all due respect, Uncle Jameson, you don't have a say in this."

"With all due respect, that ring is on my wife's finger. If you want to take it down yourself, you'll have to call the police. Does Danny know?"

A rush of emotions overwhelmed her, none of which she could label, nor did she want to sort through them. "No, and I won't tell him."

He opened the door to step inside but hesitated. "I promise this will not come back on you. I will fix it." He left her standing on the porch with the slamming of the screen.

Mirabelle dragged her feet down the sidewalk past the bags of food and climbed into the truck. Her breath fogged up the windows, but she sat there with the key in the ignition, not turning it on. Would Jameson keep his promise?

Could she keep her promise and not tell Danny? Why not? Who was he to her? And, knowing him, he'd feel compelled to report it. He'd involve law enforcement, and as large as Jameson's betrayal was, she still couldn't go that far.

Mirabelle started the engine in the empty street and turned on the defroster. She turned to face the empty seat beside her. She hadn't realized how used to having him beside her she'd grown. "Well, at least you'll believe I'm right about it being lost," she said to the empty seat he'd sat in. "Even though you were right all along."

With no dinner that night, she drove aimlessly through the streets. She should be ecstatic; the ring would be returned and she could go on with her life. Not even that thought broke through the darkness in her heart. She had a lonely life where once again the one man she relied on more than anyone had failed her.

She pulled out her phone and spotted the missing messages from the previous night, ending with the last plea: "You can trust me, Mirabelle."

Could she? She obviously couldn't trust Jameson anymore.

With a shaky hand, she picked up her phone and hit send. Even as she listened to the ring, she couldn't decide between trusting him or telling him where to go.

"Mirabelle." His voice came through with that deep understanding. "I'm glad you called. I think we can salvage this."

The dam broke, and she couldn't remember anymore the reasons to hold him back. "Good, because I need your help."

"I'm on my way."

* * * * *

Mirabelle didn't know how Danny could help her, but she wanted him beside her when she faced Bethany. Maybe she would be more apt to believe the ring had been lost at the word of an FBI agent.

Danny would have her back.

Where did that thought come from? And why did she feel so certain about it?

Whatever they decided together, she couldn't allow Jameson to return the ring. Isabelle needed him far too much, and Mirabelle would never break her aunt's heart. Whether or not she could ever forgive him, she couldn't say and wouldn't be able to for a long time. But if she didn't return the ring herself, Bethany might suspect something. To keep her reputation intact, Bethany had to believe the ring was lost and then found.

When she pulled in front of Jameson's house, Danny's car already sat out front. He stood on the porch next to a crying Isabelle.

Mirabelle pulled the latch on the truck door, popping the clutch in the process, having forgotten her engine was still running. In one movement, she yanked the keys out and shoved down the emergency brake.

Tears streaked down Isabelle's face, with Danny standing next to her with a panicked look on his face.

"What's wrong? Where's Jameson? Did you call the police on Jameson?" Panic shot through her. Had he already proven her wrong?

Isabelle jumped out of the chair. "What are you going on about, child? I was just explaining to this man that I lost my ring."

Mirabelle had reached out a hand to the porch railing about to leap up the steps. She stopped so fast she fell back a foot.

Danny took off his ball cap and took a gingerly step towards her. When had he started to wear a hat? "I just got here a few minutes ago and found Ms. Isabelle crawling around in the living room. I convinced her I'd look if she'd take a break on the porch."

"Oh, darling girl, I can't lose that ring. Why, my husband spent all his savings on it. I swear I had it this morning. You saw it."

Had Jameson left already? "Where's Uncle Jameson? Maybe he knows where it is?"

"Oh, I can't tell him. He'll be so sad."

"Why don't we look around a bit?" Danny said. "You take a break for a moment." He gestured to the house, and Mirabelle followed him, leaving Isabelle on the porch.

"Jameson stole it," she admitted as soon as the door closed behind them, the words sticking like Allie's honey to her tongue.

"No, he didn't," Danny said. "Bethany said she didn't talk to Jameson until later, and the Instagram story was posted at the start of the night. I was going through the photos, and I think he brought Isabelle."

Mirabelle glanced out the window to make sure her aunt still sat on the porch. "No, Jameson left her at home."

"Are you sure? Remember, that was the day of the storm and the power went out. Maybe he didn't want to leave her alone. Although I don't know why he'd lie about it."

She closed her eyes and nodded. "Because I told him not to bring her after last month when she got lost in the woods for a while. He must not have had anyone to stay with her but didn't want me to stress." She slapped her forehead. "Wait, Isabelle took the ring?"

"I think so."

Relief took all the strength out of her legs, but rather than finding a chair, she closed the few feet between her and Danny. She wrapped her arms around him. For a brief moment, he stood with his hands at his sides. Then he clutched her in return and held her up, giving her a sense of calm in a hurricane.

Once she found her legs again—although they were still weak, albeit for a different reason—she relinquished her grip. He held on for a second longer.

"What's wrong? I thought you'd be glad we found the ring," he asked.

"I found it this morning, and I thought Jameson stole it for Isabelle and lied to me."

"Oh." Understanding filled his face. "Oh, you thought he . . . No wonder. Look, I'll take the ring back to Bethany and tell her your horrible story about a squirrel stealing it, but we managed to find it."

"That was not a stupid story," she protested. "It could've happened."

Danny arched a brow. "Really?"

"Okay, fine, it was a dumb idea. But why are you the one who's going to take the ring back?"

"You're not a good liar, Mirabelle Mason, but I am. Every thought you have crosses your face." He brushed his fingers over her cheek.

Her cheeks warmed, wondering just how many of her thoughts he had read. Before she could chase down what it meant that he was still there, another thought took over. "You're not going to call the police?"

"Why would I do that?"

"You said if we found the person who did it, you'd—"

"You think I'd arrest some woman with Alzheimer's for picking up a ring she thought was hers?"

"No," she admitted, because she really didn't. "Thank you."

The honest truth was that she was scared by how much she'd gotten used to him, and how comfortable and uncomfortable he made her in the same moment. How she'd only known him less than a week and she wanted to ask him for help—and she didn't ask anyone for help.

With tentative fingers, she reached out to grasp his. "I'm really glad you're here." His fingers wrapped around hers.

The door burst open, and they jumped back.

Jameson stood in the doorway, a confused expression on his face. "What's going on?"

"I came to get the ring," they said simultaneously.

He glanced back and forth between the two of them. "I told you I'd handle it."

"Uncle Jameson, we know Isabelle took it."

Panic filled his face. "No, I did it as a present for her."

"Don't worry," Danny said. "Nobody's going to charge her with a crime. We'll tell Bethany we found it in the dirt, and she'll be glad to have it back."

Jameson deflated with relief. "I didn't want her to go to prison or be put in a home. She's better here."

"We know. You're the best thing for her, and she needs you."

"I can't believe you were ready to take the blame." Mirabelle threw her arms around her uncle. "What if you went to jail?"

"At least she'd have you." Jameson hugged her back.

"Where is the ring?" Mirabelle asked.

"I took it off her finger while she napped," he whispered. More shame filled his face than when he'd confessed to being a thief or when he'd told her about his money losses. "I didn't know about her having the ring until you mentioned it this morning. I left her in the truck that night, but she must've gone up the ridge and thought she found her ring. Now I have to take it away again."

Mirabelle understood immediately. Isabelle had wandered up to her and Jameson's old romantic spot. "It's okay, Jameson. She lost it once before," Mirabelle said. "She'll remember it as being lost again."

"She didn't lose it then either; I stole it." He hung his head. "It was back when my investments plunged. I took the ring off the kitchen counter while she was kneading bread and sold it." The last of that came out in a sob. "I thought I could pawn it and buy it back once the bank gave me the loan. The pawn shop gives you two weeks, but the loan didn't come through. I never told her."

Sobs overcame him, and Mirabelle stood there, doing nothing. Her breath caught, and she froze at the shock of seeing the man who'd been a rock for the entire family fall apart.

Luckily, Danny's world wasn't rocked, and he took a step forward and grasped Jameson's shoulder. "She won't know."

"No, we have to return it. Mirabelle won't pay for my mistakes."

"We'll take the ring to the jeweler and have him make a copy or order a copy or whatever. It'll be gone for a bit, and then you'll find it for her."

"Bethany has to have it by tomorrow," Jameson said. "We can't be late."

"We'll go to the jeweler now," Mirabelle said. "Then we'll call her and tell her we have it. I'm sure she'll demand we bring it to her the second she knows."

Jameson reached into his pocket and pulled out a small jewelry case containing a half-million dollars.

He passed it over to Danny, who opened the box and squinted at the ring, shaking his head. "I'll take Bethany's word about its worth." Danny handed it over to Mirabelle, who stared way too long at the ring and the man offering it to her.

Danny's phone dinged, and he read the message. "We're too late." He looked up with panic in his eyes. "The fiancé's parents came down for a surprise visit and know the ring is missing. Bethany wants to file a police report."

As if she were dying, all of Mirabelle's memories of building the business flashed before her eyes. "She's going to destroy me."

20

anny stared at his phone, contemplating the best way to respond.

"Call her," Jameson said. "Tell her we can bring it to her now."

"We can't," Danny said. "It'll look suspicious to her that she sends this message and, poof, the ring appears. She'll think you had it all along and only came forward to avoid the police."

"What do we do?" Mirabelle asked, her voice strained. "Take the ring and run to Mexico?"

"I'll ask her to hold off, that we're launching a huge search with lots of volunteers and metal detectors. Then we can tell her we found it in some gopher hole."

"I should call her," Mirabelle said.

"No," Danny burst out. "You will confess the truth in ten seconds and plead for mercy."

"I can lie."

"You can't help but be completely and totally you at every second. I'll call her on the way to the jeweler."

"Forget the jeweler," Jameson said. "Just get that woman out of our lives.”

"I will. Please, trust me on this."

Mirabelle took Danny's hand, and the warmth seeped through him on this cold morning. "It'll be okay, Uncle Jameson. We'll fix this," she said with a confidence Danny was determined to be worthy of.

Neither Danny nor Mirabelle said much on the drive to the jeweler. Mirabelle sat on the passenger seat clutching the box so hard, its edges would be engraved into her palm.

"The important thing is we have the ring. That gives us the power for now," he said.

"I know." She clutched her salvation tighter. "You know what the funny thing about all this is?"

"What's that?"

"Isabelle would've stripped that ring off her finger in a heartbeat to save Jameson. All he had to do was be honest with her."

"The hardest thing a man can admit to is failure at his job." Danny knew that better than anyone. "It's the thing that defines our identity, what gives us our value. If we can't take care of our loved ones, then what's the point?"

"How do you define yourself now?" she asked, realizing they were no longer talking about Jameson.

"I don't know." He stared through the windshield at the crowds buzzing around town. "I'm just a man doing the best he can to do the right thing."

"I've been so scared to lose myself after my two-day engagement ended. Scared of how close I came to being someone else. Even Adrien taking pictures of me and the farm for advertisements freaked me out. Like I was in risk of becoming like Bethany."

He had been so wrong about that man. "You are nothing like her."

"I know. And I'm smart enough now to not fall into the same traps as before. When I do get in a new relationship, it'll be with a man who likes me as me. I don't have to be afraid of being with someone."

Whatever happened to this woman in the next few days, she'd bounce back with or without his help. Of that, Danny had no doubt. "It's okay to ask for help," he said, "even if you don't need it. Sometimes it just feels good."

She turned to him, her eyes wide and guileless. "I needed you this week, and I'm glad I did."

Danny had once arrested several people as part of a real estate scam.

He'd found their hidden accounts and returned a good chunk of money to the victims—something that almost never happened. On the news that night, a few of victims had called him a hero. This moment trumped that. "We're here." He cleared his throat. "It looks like they're open."

The jeweler, a young man with the eagerness of a used-car salesman, beamed at them as they walked in the door. "What can I help you with? An engagement ring, perhaps?"

"Nope," Mirabelle said, grinning. "I already proposed, and the man said yes. Can you believe it?" She turned that slightly manic smile on Danny, and he realized she was punishing him for calling her a bad liar. Two could play at this game.

He draped his arm around her shoulders and pulled her towards him. "What can I say? When she knelt down, I couldn't refuse." He kissed the side of her forehead, and her entire body flinched like electricity shot through her. Hopefully, that was a good thing.

Whatever it was, she didn't pull away.

He squeezed her tighter. "Honey, show him the ring I got you." She could take credit for the proposal, but he would take credit for the bling.

Mirabelle pulled out the box and opened it. "This is a family heirloom; we were hoping you could make or find us a replica of it with fake stones."

The jeweler pulled it out and gazed into its yellow depth. "I see. You want to wear it, but also keep the original safe."

"Yes."

His face turned to confusion. "Hold on one second." He went behind the counter of sparkling jewels, pulled out a magnifying loop, and stared into the ring. When he looked up, Danny read the bad news in his expression.

His arm dropped from Mirabelle's shoulders. The game was over. "What is it?" he asked.

"This ring is made with fake diamonds. The setting looks rather recent." He stopped and waited for their reaction.

"All that, and it's fake," Mirabelle whispered. "I nearly lost everything for a fake?"

The jeweler glanced between them, obviously confused and unsure. "Do you still want the replica? I can get something ordered."

"Yes," Danny said. "We'll wait outside while you do your thing."

He hustled a stunned Mirabelle to a bench outside covered in yellow leaves. She pulled her jacket tight across her chest in the cold morning air. "I just don't understand."

Danny did, and he wished he didn't.

"Do you think Jameson . . .?" she sputtered

"No, he wouldn't have had time to make a replica."

"Then how?"

"I don't think the ring was ever real to begin with."

Her head jerked up. "Bethany put me through that for some bauble!"

"Maybe, but what I think is more likely is that she was given a replica of the original ring."

"Why?"

"The one thing that's come through from everyone this week was that her future in-laws don't like her. It's possible her fiancé not only didn't get a blessing, but he also didn't get the ring."

"What if the parents don't tell the truth? If we return a fake ring, she'll accuse of us stealing it."

"They'll have to tell the truth eventually."

"Before or after she ruins my reputation? She'll never admit to being wrong."

"She didn't notice the first time; maybe she won't notice the second. It's all about appearances for her."

"I don't know . . ."

Danny considered Bethany and her appearances. She needed a spectacle, a show. "We need a sting," he blurted out.

"A what?"

"We hide the ring in the mountains under a rock or something. Then we get as many people as possible up searching on that ridgeline with a metal detector. Instead of just telling her we found it, we invite her and her entourage to all be a part of the search." Danny jumped to his feet and pulled out his phone to find her Instagram feed. Her latest post was from the "Caribbean," even though he recognized some of the landmarks from yesterday's shoot. "It's all about perception, not reality, for her."

"We give her a story." Understanding filled Mirabelle's voice. "We give her drama. Instead of a boring proposal, she'll have this epic memory."

"Call everyone there that night and get them up on the ridge this evening. I'll get Chris and as many people as he can spare from the festival with metal detectors. I think I can convince her to meet us up there."

"Adrien can convince her. I'll have him spell it out how good it'll look. She trusts him when it comes to her image."

Danny grabbed the door of the jewelry store. "Let's get this ring and lose it in the dirt."

21

irabelle, Danny, and about fifteen other people crawled around in the dirt of the ridgeline while a few scanned the area with metal detectors. So far, they'd found eleven aluminum cans, six dollars in change, and an old raccoon trap that the sheriff had immediately shooed everyone away from.

Before the group had arrived, she and Danny had left the ring under a gray rock next to an unidentified animal hole. They wanted to wait a bit before stumbling upon it to make the sting seem legit.

Tamyra wandered back and forth through the trees with Ty behind her, asking constantly if she needed water.

Allie kept her eye on the ground while Tony furiously searched, which made Mirabelle a little nervous he'd find the ring before they did. How was it she'd missed how sleazy he was? At some point, she might have to say something to her friend about him. Maybe when she herself wasn't trying to pull something over on someone.

Bethany walked around half-heartedly kicking over rocks. After the first rush of photos with the fiancé when they first arrived, she'd quickly lost interest. They would need to act soon.

The fiancé spent most of the time on his phone, refusing to leave the one place where he'd stumbled on a signal. Occasionally, he offered a placating word to Bethany. "Babe, it's not a big deal," he said no less than three times. "Can we just go?"

"It is a big deal, and we're wasting our time up here. Your parents are blaming this on me already. We should be at the police—the real police." The tone in her voice forced everyone within earshot to suddenly become very interested in the little area of forest they scoured.

"I told you I'd buy you another ring, a better ring even than that old thing."

"That old thing represents generations of love."

Mirabelle stole a glance at the rock concealing the fake rock. They had to make this believable. So much for Danny doing all the lying for them. She'd be lucky if she got through this night without throwing up.

Speaking of throwing up, Tamyra returned from behind a tree, wiping her mouth.

Adrien came over to where Danny and Mirabelle crawled on the ground pretending to search. He joined them. "How much longer?" he whispered.

"I'd say now." She didn't look up or otherwise acknowledge him.

"I was thinking we should have the fiancé find the ring," Adrien said. "We can give him a metal detector and nudge him in the right direction."

"Won't that be kind of obvious?" Danny picked up some dirt and made a show of analyzing a handful of pebbles.

"It won't matter. It'll play great, and she'll love it."

Mirabelle nudged Danny. This was why they'd called in Adrien.

Danny stood and walked over to the one deputy who'd come with a metal detector. Mirabelle couldn't hear what they said, but after a little back-and-forth, he passed the long prod to Danny, who walked back to where the fiancé and Bethany still exchanged tense words. "I thought you'd like to try this out. Maybe the ring will be more apt to be found by its owner."

The fiancé glanced at Bethany, who shot him a death look. "Sure, why not?"

Danny showed him how to work the detector, and off he went scanning the ground.

Mirabelle came to his side. "Now what?"

"We give him a few minutes and then try to steer him in the right direction. If all else fails, I'll find it."

"This thing sucks," the fiancé declared after all of about thirty seconds.

Danny rushed to his side. "What's wrong?"

He shook it. "It's not finding anything."

"It can take a minute. Why don't you look over there?" He pointed to the rock.

Mirabelle gave off a silent prayer.

He half-heartedly ran it over the ground barely close enough to find a car, let alone a diamond ring.

"Come on," Mirabelle whispered. "Just give it half an effort."

"This is ridiculous," Bethany said. Her irritation was about to boil over.

Mirabelle moved away from the rock. "Danny, can you come help me over here for a second?"

"What is it?" he whispered into her ear once he got to her side.

"I don't want you to find it. She might think it's suspicious."

"Unless we draw him a map, that idiot—"

The detector let off a series of beeps. They both jumped at the expected but wholly welcome sound.

"What's that mean?" the fiancé asked. "Did I find it?"

The deputy went to his side while she held Danny's shirt back. "Let's see what set it off," the deputy said.

Please, please, please.

Both men knelt on the ground, and the fiancé turned over the rock. He leapt to his feet, ring in hand. "I found it. Bethany, come look."

Her face changed immediately from anger to joy. "Adrien, get over here with your camera."

Adrien rushed over while everyone else circled around to see the object that had caused so much commotion over the last week.

Bethany smiled a half-million-dollar grin while her eyes bored into her fiancé. He took the unspoken hint and once again took to his knees for the second time in a week.

A not-so-absurd thought overcame Mirabelle as she wondered if this move had been repeated in rehearsals in the weeks leading up to it.

"Bethany . . ." He took a breath. "You are the most beautiful, talented, and inspiring woman I have ever and will ever meet. Will you be my wife, again?"

Tears sprang out of Bethany's carefully lined eyes. "Of course, you doo-fus, of course." They would have to play up that she had already said yes, but he loved her so much he couldn't help but propose again.

They all clapped, again, while the two lovebirds kissed.

Bethany gazed down at the ring with a more adoring expression than the one she'd just offered her betrothed. Her look of adoring changed to confusion and then pure rage.

In that moment, Mirabelle watched all her dreams shatter.

Bethany's voice cut through the mountain air. "Hold up." She put the ring to her mouth and breathed on it like a child fogging up a window to draw on it. She pulled it back and stared. She took a step closer to Mirabelle, who refused to back down. Bethany held up the ring and dropped it onto the dirt and stomped on it. The fiancé and Danny both jumped after it, but the women never lost eye contact with each other. "Where's the real ring?"

"I don't know," Mirabelle said without a quiver in her voice. "But that's the ring you lost."

"You think you could replace the real one with a fake and I wouldn't notice? You think I wouldn't know the second that cheap metal hit my hand? I suspected you would try to pull something like this." Bethany had obviously, but mistakenly, trusted her fiancé more than them.

"That's the ring you had a week ago. If it's fake, then ask your fiancé about it."

Bethany's hand swung around, but Mirabelle took a step back and caught the slap in her own palm. Rage ran through Bethany's eyes. "I will bring charges against you, and your little errand boy won't stop me." She sneered at Danny, who'd closed the gap between the two of them to stop whatever was coming. "Destroying your company will be the least of your worries."

Danny turned to the fiancé. "Tell her," he pleaded with him. "Tell her you gave her a copy."

His desperate glance shot between Danny and Bethany. "Babe, I would never have given you a fake ring, but I don't know if it's worth reporting it to the police. We can get it—"

"No," she snarled. "She's already destroyed my perfect moment, twice. I should've done it a week ago. People like her can't be trusted."

"I can get you another one, a better one."

Bethany's skin reddened to an almost purple as she raged at Mirabelle.

"What? Did you think you could steal my life by stealing my ring? Little nothings like you are always trying to tear down people like me. I'm sorry I'm worth more than you, okay? But that doesn't give you the right . . ."

She kept going on, but Mirabelle didn't flinch and dug her boot heel into the dark dirt. "I don't need to tear you down. I don't need your review. I've built my own business and my own reputation. Go ahead and tell the world your lies. Even if I have to close down my stable, I'll build up something else in its place. My life isn't built on a fake product."

Bethany's mouth opened to scream out her indignities.

"Report it to the police," Mirabelle continued, with no tremor in her voice this time. "Then call his parents and tell them about the ring. See if they still want to press charges over a cubic zirconia worth a few hundred dollars." She reached into her pocket and yanked out a hundred-dollar bill—a tip from a grateful client. "Here," she said, tossing it on the ground next to the scuffed ring. "This is for your troubles."

Bethany lunged at her, but her fiancé's arms held her back.

Chris jumped in between them. "Let's go down to the sheriff's office and get this sorted out."

"Wait!" Danny yelled. "Adrien, do you have the photos of the ring?"

Adrien shoved his camera into the fray. "I have pictures of the ring on your finger right after the engagement. We can compare the rings."

Bethany tore the camera out of her hands, and Mirabelle hoped it wouldn't join the ring on the ground in a broken heap.

"Look close," Danny said. "One thing I noticed when I first saw the photos was how good of a condition the ring was for being an heirloom."

"Tell her the truth; it's all going to come out sooner or later," Mirabelle said to the fiancé.

Bethany whipped around to glare at the man who'd put the ring on her finger. "You didn't."

He reached out to caress her face, but she batted his hand away. "Come on, beautiful; don't be like that. Mother and Dad wouldn't give me the ring when I told them I was going to propose. And you said, Bethany, it had to be that ring or no ring."

She opened and closed her mouth.

"It just seemed easier to lie. What's it matter?"

"It matters because every woman in your family has worn that ring for five generations," she pleaded. She kicked the yellow ring out of the dirt and over the edge of the ridge. "If I don't have that one, then everyone will think I'm not enough."

"But you are. You're the most beautiful girl I've ever seen." She turned away from him, and he sighed. "What do you want, then? The fake one, or a real one I buy?"

She glanced down the ridge and back to him, as if this was the hardest decision she'd ever had to face. "Fine," she said. "You'll buy me a new ring, but it had better be bigger and worth an easy million."

He shrugged as if that was no amount at all. "Fine. It was embarrassing to have you wearing an old ring anyhow, like I wasn't my own man."

"Are we square, then?" Mirabelle asked Bethany.

The influencer looked her up and looked her down. "Yes, but I'm not posting any of your photos." She turned to Adrien. "We'll need an entirely new proposal shoot with the new ring. I'm thinking an ocean theme with sapphires." She strode down the trail, leaving everyone standing there, mouths agape.

Mirabelle's legs almost gave out, and she grabbed a tree branch to steady her.

"You can have the copy ring if you can find it," the fiancé said. "It only cost a few thousand bucks."

"Thanks," she said automatically, still trying to process everything that had happened.

He turned to leave.

"Hey," Danny called out to the fiancé. "I never did get your name."

"Brandon," he said, and he took down the trail after his ill-chosen future.

"What?" Danny said to Mirabelle's quizzical look. "It's been driving me nuts. No one ever called him anything but 'fiancé.'"

Chris and his deputy packed up the metal detector and took to the trail.

"You okay?" Tamyra asked.

She nodded, still in shock that it was all over. "Go ahead. I'll be down in a minute."

Everyone cleared out except Danny.

She sank down on the nearest boulder, which also happened to be the boulder where the ring had been lost.

He sat next to her. "It is a beautiful sunset," he said, staring out over the horizon.

For the first time, she failed to appreciate its beauty, and instead she turned her attention to the man beside her. "It's the last week of the festival," she said.

"Yes, it is."

"And that means you'll be going."

He took his eyes off the streaks of pink crisscrossing the sky. "What are you doing the first Friday in November?" Danny finally asked.

"Probably sleeping. Why?"

"Would you like to go on a date with me?"

She grinned. "My first weekend off all season? I suppose I can move some things around, but—"

His lips didn't let hers finish the argument.

Epilogue

One Year Later

t was the last night of the festival, and Mirabelle released the last horse
to its stall, heralding the end of another season. Exhaustion threatened
to overwhelm her, but she still had to feed and get the yard cleaned up.
The clouds warned of an overnight storm, and she wanted to bring in the
bales to keep them from getting rained on.

She walked out through the bright red barn doors, painted by her and
Danny the previous spring as soon as the days were warm enough. Every
night that season had been sold out. She would use the extra money to build
a new building next door to the barn for events; she could host parties,
dances, and whatever else people wanted.

Danny was already in the yard, picking up the first bale. "How did it
go?" he asked.

"They said they'd never seen a sunset so pretty. And get this: a couple
got engaged."

"Please tell me she still has the ring."

"Yes, but it was close. He was so nervous he dropped it. Both Uncle Jameson and I lunged for it and almost caught it before it hit the ground."

He roared with laughter. "Glad I wasn't there."

She reached up and straightened the collar of his uniform. "How was your evening, Deputy? Did you get stuck on festival duty the entire night?"

"Of course, newest man on the totem pole and all that." He'd figured out the winter before that he didn't need to be solving billion-dollar cases or earning tons of his own money to be worth something. He just needed to be saving the day for someone. "You know I'm a hero," he said. "I tracked down a stolen wallet for an eighty-year-old woman, and those are the very words she used."

He spoke facetiously, but she could see the pride in him. "I hope you told her you're spoken for."

He winked. "Am I?"

She ignored the bait, knowing that would get under his skin in a good way. "I do miss your old security guard uniform. Something about a man in khaki." She turned to the barn, but he grabbed her shirt and pulled her in for a kiss, and she did not refuse. He pulled back after a few seconds, but she tugged him closer for more, savoring his nearness and his strong arms wrapped around her for a moment longer before releasing him.

Their first date had turned into multiple, and she loved the easy way he settled in with her friends and she with his. Even Aunt Isa, who could never remember his name, called him "that sweet fellow of yours."

"I hope you didn't come all the way out here at this time of night just for that. I need some help getting these bales in." She turned back to the barn.

"Mirabelle."

"What?" she said without turning, thinking of all the saddles that would need to be cleaned the next day before being stored for winter.

"I didn't come just to help you move bales."

She turned. "If you think I'm going—"

He'd knelt on the ground. "I would've brought you a ring, but you said . . ."

For a moment she froze in absolute shock before nodding quickly, desperate to keep the tears from overflowing.

"So I only brought you me, and I hope that's enough." He held his empty hands out, offering her everything she could want. "Will you marry me?"

Of course he was enough; he was more than enough. But being with him in the last year had convinced her of the one thing she'd always doubted, that she could be enough for a man. They were each other's enough.

With no photographer, videographer, or cheering crowd, there was only him and her and the life they were building together.

"Okay," she said with an impish smile. "Why not?"

He swept her up again.

Check out the next in the series!

Honeycombs and Homecomings

The Author

Melissa is an analyst by day, writer by night, and adventurer by weekend. All of that makes her sound way more awesome than she is, but that's the point. Most of her stories include some outdoor element since that's where her best ideas come from. Follow her adventures at weekendwomanwarrior.com.

For updates and deals on books, sign up for her newsletter:
https://mailchi.mp/1a0cfaa61f57/weekend-woman-warrior

9 798696 213552